Tomorrow's Child

Tomorrow's Child

Family Tangles: A New Spin on Some Ancient Tales

Jennifer Johnson

TOMORROW'S CHILD
Copyright © 2017, Jennifer Johnson
Trade Paperback ISBN: 978-1-946608-04-8
eBook ISBN: 978-1-946608-3

Cover Art Design by El Roi WW

Digital Release, April 2017
Trade Paperback Release, April 2017

Media > Books > Fiction > Romance Novels
Categories:

TOMORROW'S CHILD

He may be the only person who can save her daughter's life.

Five years ago, Dr. Tamara Wallace made a decision to have the child she'd always wanted. Now her daughter has leukemia. And the only man who can save Miranda's life won't return Tamara's phone calls.

Nicolaus Pack thought he'd put the pain and grief of losing his son behind him, but when a woman approaches him to be a stem cell donor, he realizes his son may have left a legacy that could bring more heart ache or be the healing he's needed all along.

"She is more righteous than I."

Genesis 38: 26

CHAPTER ONE

What do you say to a man to get him to open his vein and give you his blood?

Tamara crossed her legs in the elegant but impersonal waiting room and contemplated that question.

Hello. I'm Tamara Wallace. Would you mind undergoing a medical procedure for someone you've never met before?

Tamara had Googled Nicolaus Pack. What she read didn't give her much hope that he was going to help her. But Tamara had to try. Her entire future rested on her ability to elicit compassion in a man who made his living putting his feelings aside in the name of justice.

Oh, Nicolaus Pack. Please help me. Please help my baby.

"Tamara Wallace."

Tamara stood up and walked in front of the secretary's desk. "It's pronounced Tah-mara. The emphasis is on the second syllable. It sounds like *Tomorrow*. Tamara Wallace." She wouldn't make such a big deal about it except she'd explained it when she first came in two hours ago.

The woman's eyebrow arched. Tamara looked at her

nameplate. Jessica Adams. Not too many ways one could mispronounce *that* name. "I'm sorry. Mr. Pack is not going to be able to meet with you today."

"I have an appointment, and I've been waiting two hours." Tamara was proud of herself for not whining about the horrible way Nicolaus Pack was behaving, as if her time didn't matter. Well, certainly, it didn't matter to him. That was obvious.

"If you could just tell me what this is about."

Nope. Tamara wasn't sure what she'd say to Nicolaus if she were even able to speak to him. Trying to communicate through his secretary was not the way to go. "It's a personal matter."

Her eyebrow lifted. "This is Mr. Pack's place of business. He doesn't conduct personal matters here."

"If I could reach him at home, I would."

"I'm sorry, Ms. Wallace." The woman stared at her.

"I can hire him as my lawyer. I will pay him for his time, if that's the issue. Then it will be business."

She shook her head. "No."

Who does she think I am? An ex-girlfriend? Hardly. She had never seen the man, but Tamara was guessing by the set-up of his office, he liked young leggy blondes, not forty-something overworked doctors. Yes, she was judging the man. But his present action of not giving her the time of day, while robbing several hours of hers wasn't sitting well.

"This is my name and number," Tamara said taking a piece of paper from her purse and writing on it. "Would you give this to him? He can call or text me."

The secretary accepted the card and placed it on her desk without looking at it. "I will put it in his inbox, yes."

Tamara wondered if that was code for throwing it in the trash after she left the room. Nodding, Tamara placed her purse strap on her shoulder. "Thank you." She walked toward the door and opened it, exiting the offices of Pack, Bryan, and Levine.

I've got to see him, but how?

Tamara had tried calling, but hadn't even been able to reach his personal secretary. She thought if she made an appointment with him, she'd at least have the chance to speak to him face to face. Her mistake had been that she'd said it was personal and not business.

She walked toward the elevator and pressed the down button. The lit number on the panel indicated it was on the ground floor. A nearby window provided a view of downtown, and Tamara stepped over to it, studying the overcast day. She didn't like being in the city. It was a violent place, stabbings and shootings on the news every night. Why would he have his office here anyway?

A slight twinge in her eye caused her to blink. Stupid contacts. She hated wearing them. Tamara lifted her hand and pinched her eyelid hoping to readjust the contact, then blinked again. Her eye teared. Great. She'd have raccoon eyes thanks to the mascara.

A door opened down the corridor, and Tamara heard purposeful footsteps approaching—two sets. She wiped the skin beneath her eye and noticed the black smudge on the end of her finger. She wiped again with another finger.

"Call Springer and see if we can reschedule for four o'clock Tuesday, and I want you to go to the courthouse and go to the records division. Look for anything from April for Fitzpatrick at the address we have."

Two men appeared and stood in front of the elevator. Both in business suits, the younger one frantically pushed on the screen of an electronic pad while the older man spoke. He glanced at her before turning his attention to the elevator buttons, and Tamara's heart thumped hard in her chest.

He had the same color eyes as her daughter.

Butterflies fluttered in her stomach, and she took a steadying breath. It could be the situation making her nervous. Certainly meeting her daughter's grandfather could cause a physiological reaction. Or asking him to go through a medical procedure so the granddaughter he didn't know he had could live. Anyone would react with an elevated heartbeat. Probably elevated blood pressure, too, if the warmth in her face was any indication.

This had to be Nicolaus Pack.

Wow. He was younger than she expected. Probably close to her own age. He must have had Reginald when he was in his late teens or early twenties, whereas Tamara was forty when Miranda was born.

Tamara closed the distance between them. "Hello."

"Hello," he returned, not looking at her again.

The younger man nodded at her.

"Are you Nicolaus Pack?"

His mouth tightened in a grim line.

"I had an appointment with you."

"I'm sorry." His finger pushed the down button. "Something came up, and it's very important." His voice was deep, almost melodic. Yes, she could imagine him in a courtroom. That timbre of voice would command respect, attention.

"Your son Reginald—"

"Is dead. I'm sorry if he owed you money. I don't pay his debts."

"Yes, I know. About his death, I mean. I'm sorry for your loss."

He pushed the elevator button again.

"He doesn't owe me money. It's nothing like that. He… Reginald is…was the father of my daughter."

He laughed and shook his head, not even bothering to look at her. "Nice try, but I don't think so."

Tamara didn't take it personally. Reginald had been nineteen years old when he had made the donation. At twenty, he had become a father, though he hadn't known it. Tamara wasn't cougar material. She'd gained thirty pounds when she was pregnant, and hadn't lost it though Miranda was four.

"He was a sperm donor at a bank. I never met him."

Nicolaus didn't have the decency to glance her way. "You're delusional, lady, and you're also barking up the wrong family tree."

The elevator door opened, and he stepped inside. "Please take the next elevator. I'm very busy, and I don't have time to play Kardashians with you." The younger man followed him in and turned around to face the front, blocking Tamara's view of Nicolaus Pack. The other man shot an apologetic look at Tamara.

"She has leukemia. Please if you would just—"

The door closed.

Dammit.

****

Tamara sat at the kitchen table with Sandra, her mother, and her best friend Charlotte. After putting Miranda to bed, Tamara had come into the kitchen to see both of them sitting at the table with cups of steaming tea. A third cup waited for her at her chair.

Obviously, they wanted to know what had happened at the meeting between her and Miranda's grandfather. Tamara was sure they could tell it hadn't gone well, though Tamara had tried to hide the devastation she felt.

What am I going to do?

Miranda might die if she didn't get a donation of stem cells or bone marrow.

Tamara sat down. She watched her hands hug the cup, her fingers warmed by the ceramic sides.

"Well?" Charlotte asked. "What did he say?"

"He said no." Tamara found the courage to look at their faces. Sandra's quivering lip caused her attention to scurry to Charlotte. The angry expression was easier to deal with.

"How could he say no? What kind of monster is he?"

"I don't know. He wouldn't even meet with me."

"I thought you had an appointment. How come it took you so long?"

"I waited two hours in his office, then his secretary informed me he wasn't going to talk to me. I saw him in the hall outside of his office, but he blew me off."

"Didn't you have the chance to say anything to him?"

"I told him he had a grandchild, but it didn't matter. He didn't believe me. He called me delusional."

"Well, it does sound like something from a soap opera."

"I mentioned Reginald, and you should have seen his face. It was as if he turned into a statue."

"Who is Reginald?" Charlotte asked.

"Reginald was the name of the sperm donor. He died in a car wreck last year. Nicholas Pack is his father," Sandra supplied.

"He was so hostile. He thought I had come to him because Reginald owed me money. He said he doesn't pay Reginald's debts."

"Well, he sure ought to pay this one," Charlotte declared.

"What does he mean by paying Reginald's debts? Do you think Reginald was a gambler?" Tamara's mother asked.

"Oh, my gosh. What if he was? Could Miranda inherit the gambling trait?"

Tamara rubbed the bridge of her nose. "Not helpful, Charlotte."

"Sorry." She ducked her head as she brought the teacup to her mouth and sipped. "Did he outright say he wouldn't get tested?"

"We didn't even get that far. He thought I was there for money. Then when I told him Reginald was Miranda's biological father, he laughed in my face."

"What a prick."

That, from Charlotte.

"Anyway, I told him Miranda has leukemia, and he didn't even let me finish. He walked into the elevator, told me he was too busy to deal with me."

"Why didn't you follow him onto the elevator?"

"He told me not to. I should have, but honestly, I was so shocked. I couldn't believe how cold he was."

"How awful. Who would refuse to help a little girl?"

"Well." Tamara shook her head. "I want to give him the benefit of the doubt. You know how shocking it would be to find out you have a grandchild because your son had gone to a sperm bank? Anyone would freak out about it. I probably shouldn't have sprung it on him, but he didn't give me much choice. He kept me waiting two hours just to see him, and then bailed on me. He made me feel like I was a…a prostitute who had offered him a good time in a back alley somewhere."

"What a horrible man."

"He sounds just like a lawyer. You sure he doesn't do personal injury?"

"I don't know. I didn't ask him. I didn't get the chance."

"So, what are you going to do?"

"I don't know. Maybe we can find another marrow donor or Nicolaus Pack might change his mind." Tamara didn't like having everything hinge on a donor, and especially not someone like him. It was possible that Miranda's cancer would go into remission with the chemo, but her chances of a complete recovery were so much better with the marrow.

Tamara had had so many plans before all of this had happened. She'd completed her residency and had the position at the hospital. She'd wanted to try to get pregnant again. In fact, she'd had her first appointment at the clinic the day before Miranda had gotten sick. The timing seemed ironic, then maybe providential. But Reginald's sperm was no longer available. She'd found that out when she'd gone to the clinic. Tamara had let go of having another baby until Miranda could be cured. Miranda's health was the only thing that mattered now

The only thing.

****

Trauma alert. ETA Eight minutes.

Tamara's beeper sounded. She removed it from the waistband of her scrub pants, and looked at the small screen which gave a brief description of the kind of trauma, the gender and age of the patient, and the estimated time of arrival in minutes.

MVC. Priority 2. 61 male 8 minutes by ground.

Motor Vehicle Crash. 61 year old male who would arrive by ambulance in 8 minutes. Priority 2 meant it wasn't immediately life-threatening.

The trauma team would have received messages on their pagers. Soon, they would crowd into the ER to wait on the patient who would arrive through the sliding glass door at the ambulance entrance.

Tamara's cell phone rang, and she picked it up from the desktop and examined the screen. It was Charlotte.

"Are you on call tonight?" Charlotte launched into the conversation without a greeting.

"No."

"Oh, good because I've bought you a plane ticket. I want to you fly down here. You get off at seven, right?"

Tamara shook her head at her best friend Charlotte's statement. "Why in the world would I want to go to a law conference in Atlanta? I don't have time for this. I've got one more hour on the clock, and they just called a trauma in that should be here in seven minutes."

"He's here."

"Who?"

"Nicolaus Pack."

"Oh. Well, so what?"

"You can talk to him, Tamara. I can help you."

Tamara studied the clock on the wall. Six minutes until the trauma arrived.

"What makes you think he would talk to me now when he wasn't even willing to ride an elevator with me a month ago?"

"This is too good of an opportunity to pass up. I mean, what are the chances, you know? You could tell him about Miranda—what an incredible little girl she is. You could convince him to be tested for being a donor without his secretary getting in your way."

Two weeks ago, Tamara had sent him two pictures of Miranda with a note. *This is your granddaughter Miranda. She has a rare form of leukemia. Your blood could save her life.*

Tamara had included the name and address of the organization where Reginald had registered making his identity available for any biological children he had. She had included her own contact information and a brief description of the blood test and the procedure for both a peripheral blood stem cell and a bone marrow donation. It was possible if he were a match, he'd only have to give a pint of his blood. It was no worse than when a person gave platelets.

She had heard nothing from him. Nothing.

Tamara turned and glanced into bay two where the rest of the medical staff were gathering to wait for the trauma patient.

Four minutes. Time was running out.

"I can't fly down to Atlanta. I have to work tomorrow."

"Your return flight is five o'clock tomorrow morning and be back at work by seven."

"Are you kidding?"

"I didn't want you to use the excuse that you couldn't come because you had to work."

Tamara shook her head. "No, Charlotte. This is too crazy. Showing up there on the off chance that I can convince him to listen to me?"

"It isn't crazy. It's perfect. I'll pick you up at the airport and fill you in on the details on our way. It'll be fine. Really."

"I don't want to spend the night away from Miranda. I'm switching to evenings in a few weeks, and I don't have that many nights left to be with her when she goes to sleep."

"Don't you see? You're doing this for her, and you'll be back home tomorrow."

Tamara shook her head. "No, Charlotte. I think it's a bad idea."

"Oh, just wait. I've got an even better idea."

"What?"

"I'll tell you when you get here."

Chapter Two

Tamara sat in the passenger side of the car watching in amazement as Charlotte zipped along I-75 like she was a NASCAR driver.

"When are you ovulating?" Charlotte asked.

"What? Why?"

"Because I was thinking if Nicolaus isn't willing to give bone marrow, maybe we could get another kind of donation from him if you're fertile."

A suspicion blew up like a dynamite charge in Tamara's mind at what Charlotte's scheme was. If Charlotte was interested in Tamara's ovulation, she could only be thinking about Tamara getting pregnant, and Nick being the donor.

And the purpose of getting pregnant would be to produce a donor for Miranda. The chances Nick would help her produce a matching donor were so much better than the fertility clinic. But if he wouldn't give her marrow, why would he agree to donating sperm?

"Don't be ridiculous. First of all, if he won't even talk to me about a blood donation, what in the world would make you think he'd be willing to father a child? Good grief, Charlotte, how can you think such a thing?"

"You told me yourself you'd gone to the fertility clinic when Miranda got sick. But what if you didn't have to go to the clinic? And what if the baby was a match for Miranda?"

"I couldn't even get him to agree to meet with me. He isn't going to agree to a sperm donation."

"Maybe not, but what if he agreed to a one night stand?"

Tamara shot a glance at her friend. "On the chance that I would get pregnant? Even if I did, do you know how unlikely it is that the baby would be a genetic match? People who have had donor babies do so by preimplantation genetic diagnosis. Otherwise, they have little chance of getting a match."

"Pre what?"

Tamara breathed out a frustrated sigh. "They decide which embryo has the correct characteristics and implant it in the uterus. Setting aside the unethical implications of tricking a man into becoming a father...."

"Women have done that for centuries," Charlotte argued. "And anyway, you'd never have to see him again after tonight. He'd never know."

"It's wrong."

"If it provides a donor for Miranda, it isn't wrong. The end justifies the means. Absolutely, it does, and you know if it would provide a donor for her, you'd do it."

"I don't think it's right."

"You'd love the baby. Nicholas Pack would never know. You'd have a sibling for Miranda. It's perfect."

Tamara shook her head.

"Okay, fine. Forget about it then, but I think it's worth considering. This conference is the legal equivalent to Sodom and Gomorrah. You've got the perfect venue for something like this. Well, nearly perfect, anyway."

"What do you mean?"

"I've been trying to butter up Granddaddy Pack to carry out the diabolical plan, but he seems to be the only attorney attending who does not imbibe in the sexual nectar of Hotlanta."

Tamara smiled. "Is present company also excluded?"

Charlotte shot her a seductive smile. "When in Rome, baby. We work hard all year long, and this is our chance to play extra hard. I love this conference." She wrinkled her nose. "I think Mr. Pack needs to drop his pants and do his duty."

Tamara shivered. "I'm not on board with your plan. And besides, you've seen how attractive he is. There is no way Nicolaus Pack would want to sleep with me."

"Don't sell yourself short. If you'd lose those glasses and take your hair out of that ponytail, maybe you'd get a date."

"Who would want me? I'm a forty-four-year-old single mother whose last sexual experience was in college, and I live with my mother."

"Your mother lives with you, and that's just because of your crazy work schedule, and you're a doctor for goodness' sake. I don't know why men aren't beating down the door to let you play doctor with them."

Tamara smiled. "Yeah, I can just hear it. 'Oh, Tamara, it's such a turn-on when you probe the laceration on my head to remove the broken glass then come at me with a surgical needle to suture me.' 'Oh, Tamara, I scream in pleasure when you set my fractured tibia'."

"Oh, Tamara, I love it when you stick that twelve inch catheter tube in my peepee," Charlotte crooned.

Tamara laughed. "Hey, catheter placement is the nurse's honor. Not mine."

"So, how are we going to hook you and Nicolaus Pack up?"

"I don't want to hook up with him. But I do want the chance to talk to him without his secretary running interference. Where have you been meeting him?"

"He was in the same seminar I was in Thursday afternoon, and I stalked him to the bar last night. We had a couple of drinks, and I was hopeful, but then some of the girls from corporate law dragged me off with some jell-o shots, and he was gone when I came back. At lunch today, I saw him again, and I gave him my phone number. He looked at it and put it in his breast pocket. That's when I bought your airplane ticket, because putting my number in the pocket closest to his heart means he is a definite score. But tonight, he told me he wasn't interested in having an affair even though if he was, I would be top on his list."

"How very diplomatic of him."

"The problem is you're wearing that, so you're not going to blend in."

That was a pair of green scrubs and her winter coat. She had worn them to work and hadn't had time to change.

"I wish I had thought to buy some clothes at the airport."

"Maybe he'll have a heart attack, and you can give him CPR."

"Only 17% of people who have a cardiac arrest survive it with CPR outside of the hospital so don't wish that fantasy on Miranda's grandfather. I'd love the chance for him to give her that marrow."

"We have to convince him first."

"I wonder if he's a breakfast person."

"You'll need to catch an Uber early tomorrow. I'm thinking no later than five am in case you want to get home and freshen up before work. I doubt anyone eats breakfast before five."

"This is impossible. What were you thinking?"

"I was thinking I could get you laid tonight and on a plane in the morning before your shift."

"You're hopeless."

"Hopeful." Charlotte exited the interstate and maneuvered the car into the parking lot of the convention center. "Here we are. What do you think of just going up to his room? Gang up on him?"

"I don't know."

Charlotte parked the car and cut the engine. The women left the vehicle and walked side by side to the front of the Peachtree Conference Center. "This place is huge," Tamara commented.

"Yeah. Had to be to fit all the egos." She held out her hand to Tamara. "Here's the room card. I'll go in the bar and look for him." Charlotte marched across the lobby and disappeared down a hallway.

A few minutes later in the hotel room, Tamara shrugged out of her coat and hung it in the closet. She shut the mirrored door and walked into the main room, picking up the remote lying on one of the beds. She aimed it at the set and surfed through the channels.

What am I doing here?

Shouldn't I be downstairs looking for him?

A scene popped on the television of one of her favorite movies from her youth—ah, the teenage angst. She'd seen it at least a hundred times when she was in junior high school.

Her phone dinged, signaling a text, probably from her partner in crime.

Tamara looked at the screen.

Finishing his drink. Looks like he's calling it a night. Get down here.

Her heart sped up. She grabbed her pack and put her phone in it, then shouldered it as she scrambled out of the room.

Charlotte was waiting for her at the corner of the hallway she'd disappeared down just a few minutes ago. She looked behind her than hurried toward Tamara. They met in the middle of the lobby.

"He'll take the stairs. I've seen him do it every time he goes up to his room. He must have a phobia of elevators."

"Or maybe he's on the same floor as you and thinks one flight of stairs is not too much to walk."

Charlotte wrinkled her nose at her friend. "I followed him to his room last night. He's on the third floor. Why are you defending him?"

Tamara shrugged. She had seen the man willingly enter an elevator on the tenth floor. Maybe he was attempting to avoid her, but he hadn't shown any anxiety when he'd asked her not to ride the elevator with him.

"So, anyway, just keep a lookout for him. He shot me down once again, and had signaled the waitress for his bill." Charlotte pointed to a door. "That's the stairwell door. Mark my word, he'll take the stairs."

"So, what? I corner him in the stairwell? Are you going to help me?"

Charlotte shook her head. "He sees me, he'll smell a rat for sure. If he won't talk to you in the stairwell, just go on up to the third floor. Text me, and I'll meet you up there. He's staying in room 323. We'll knock on his door and gang up on him."

"And probably get arrested."

"You can make him listen to you. I know you can."

"He didn't listen to me when I had an appointment with him."

"That was his home turf. This is neutral territory. You're on even ground here." Charlotte patted her shoulder. "We have to get him to listen to you, or else I'll knock him in the head and you can...you know." She grinned and walked to the elevator.

Tamara waited for a moment, then walked up to the front desk. A young woman in a green blazer smiled at her. "Hello," she said. "May I help you?"

"I left my toothbrush and toothpaste at home. Do you have any extras?"

"Certainly."

****

Nick stalked to the stairwell door, the solitude of his room awaiting him. He'd had enough of the cutthroats and piranhas at this conference. And that was just the women.

He'd be flying out in the morning and back at the office by his ten am appointment.

A woman in scrubs reached the doorway a second before he did. He grasped the door handle and opened it, stepping back so she could enter. She stopped and stared at him, her narrowed gaze assessing him.

"I usually take the stairwell," he said.

She nodded and walked through, and he waited a beat before he followed. She grasped the rail and began to ascend, but paused at the bottom stair pivoting her body to face him. "Why?"

"Excuse me?"

"Why do you usually take the stairwell?" Her voice echoed in the chamber.

What was she doing here? Obviously, she wasn't an

attorney. Her outfit made her stick out like a sore thumb. "Taking the stairs is good for my heart, so my doctor tells me. My name's Nick. What's yours?"

She studied him for a couple of seconds. "Tomorrow."

"What?"

'You asked me my name, and I said, Tomorrow."

Nick chuckled for the first time in months. "Why do I feel as if I'm in a Laurel and Hardy routine?"

She blinked at him then began to mount the stairs, and he followed her. She wore a small backpack. She must use it instead of carrying a purse. He judged her to be about forty years old, with a nice ass. He could tell even with her loose pants. Following her on the stairs provided him a damn good view.

She shot him a smile over her shoulder. "Go ahead and joke or even break into song. I've heard it all before."

"So, Tomorrow, are you in the medical profession? Is what my doctor telling me correct?"

"Yes, and yes."

"Amazing. Someone who isn't an attorney. I thought the hotel was full with the legal convention."

"I have some family business I needed to take care of. The hotel was close to the airport, and they found a place for me to sleep."

They were reaching the landing. Tomorrow might provide some answers about his granddaughter, if he could talk her into having a drink with him. Too bad they were headed in the wrong direction to do that. "Have you been to the bar yet?"

"Umm, no."

"I just came from there. Would you like to go back down and have a drink with me? I'd like the chance to talk to someone about anything other than law."

Her shoe missed the top step, and she stumbled. Nick wasn't quick enough to catch her before she fell forward on the floor, a crack accompanying the fall. A cellophane wrapped toothbrush and a small tube of toothpaste skittered across the tile. Nick knelt to help her. Her glasses were askew on her nose, and she straightened them before reaching for the items she'd dropped, crouching low to the floor in an attempt to retrieve them.

Nick picked up them up and handed them to her. "Are you okay?"

She closed her eyes, an expression of pain flitted across her face, and then it was gone. "Yes."

She attempted to stand, and Nick put his arm around her waist and helped her to her feet.

"Are you sure?"

She shifted her weight on her right side and flinched. "I'm okay. I just twisted my ankle, I think."

"Where's your room?"

"This floor. 212." She took a step and stopped, gripping his arm.

"Maybe you ought to see a doctor."

She laughed.

"What? You don't like doctors?"

"I am a doctor."

"Really? I thought doctors wore white coats. You look more like a nurse."

"I've got my stethoscope in my pack. Not that it proves anything, but then again I'm not at work right now." She breathed in, then out and straightened. She walked a few steps, and Nick matched her pace. He opened the door, and they went through.

"You're really a medical doctor? What kind?"

"ER."

"Impressive. You must be good in crisis situations."

"It's easier to have a level head when someone else is having the crisis."

"Good point. I'll help you to your room."

"Thanks."

She limped, but it was slight. He surmised she was trying to hide it, as she took measured slow steps. She was a doctor. Great. She could answer medical questions. That's what he needed. Her fingers loosened on his sleeve, and he tightened his hold on her. He felt her softness through the thin material of her clothes.

They stopped at the door, and she reached her fingers into the pocket of her shirt, drawing Nick's attention to her breasts. Because of the cut of the scrubs, he couldn't see any cleavage, but he knew she had some. Even the cut of the shirt couldn't hide the size of her impressive rack.

He'd noticed, too, she had no jewelry on her hands. No wedding ring. Women were married by her age.

Or divorced.

Or maybe she didn't wear jewelry because of her profession. You couldn't sew people up in the emergency room if you had on rings, could you?

She had retrieved the key card from her pocket, but it slipped through her fingers and fell to the floor. "I don't know what's wrong with me. I'm usually not this clumsy."

Nick bent to retrieve the card, noticing her shoes. Clunky hospital shoes. All he'd seen the women here wear since the conference started were knee high riding boots and insanely high heeled pumps.

Nick slipped the card in the slot and opened the door. He held it open for her. She switched on the lights and glanced around the room. He saw no personal items there except for a laptop on the table in the corner.

"Do you drink wine?" he asked.

She shrugged out of the pack and laid it on the dresser. Walking to the bed, she folded the comforter back. "On occasion."

Her actions made him pause. Was she getting in bed? How interesting.

"I'm going to elevate my ankle. Would you mind getting some ice?"

"Not at all."

Nick found the ice bucket on the counter next to the sink. He stopped at the door and looked back at her. She stood next to the bed and fluffed a pillow then placed it at the foot of the bed. Something about her—Nick couldn't put his finger on it—she seemed familiar somehow. He didn't know why.

"I'll be back in a few minutes," he said.

She paused and turned toward him. Her eyes glimmered, or was it the light reflecting on the lens of her glasses?

"Is your husband with you on this trip?"

Her lips lifted in a smile. "I'm not married."

"Are you wondering if I am?"

"Since you asked me in the stairwell if I'd have a drink with you, I'd like to think you're not."

"I'm not."

She sat on the bed and scooted back against the headboard. "Thank you, Nick, for bringing me the ice."

She was reminding him of the task she'd assigned him, he was pretty sure.

He was about to ask her for her card key and remembered he had tucked it in his pocket when he'd let them in. He needed to remember to return it. The door clicked shut behind him and he strode down the hallway. Instead of stopping at the ice machine in the small snack room at the end of the corridor, he went to the doorway to the stairs and headed down to the bar.

The bartender wouldn't give him a bottle and two glasses, but she did let him place an order which would be brought up by room service. Nick was about to leave when he caught sight of a woman he'd met a few days ago making a beeline toward him.

Oh dammit. He didn't want to fool with her right now. She'd come on to him earlier like a bitch in heat.

"Hi Nicolaus. I've been looking for you," she said.

He didn't bother to look at her. "Hi, Charlotte."

"Listen, if you're not busy, why don't we go somewhere a little more private. It's really loud in here."

"Like I told you, I'm not looking to hook up with anyone." He began to walk away, but she caught his arm and fell into step beside him.

"I know. I totally understand. I just wanted to talk about...law. After all, isn't that why we're really here?"

Nick stopped and extricated her hand from his elbow. The woman had on zebra print that looked like it had been melted and poured on her. "You want to go somewhere private and talk about law... in that dress?"

She grinned. "I might as well give you something nice to look at while we decide what the Supreme Court is going to do about the public social media case."

Animal prints tended to give him a headache.

He thought he'd made his feelings perfectly clear earlier tonight, but apparently the sweet young thing didn't take a hint very well.

Thankfully, Charlotte's cell phone dinged and she looked at the screen. Her eyes widened, and her fingers flew across the screen. For the moment, she forgot Nick, which was a great opportunity for him to get away.

He exited the bar without any further incident and was back in Tomorrow's room with the promised bucket of ice.

Tomorrow, what a crazy and cool name.

She lounged on the bed, her back pressed against several pillows and her leg propped on more pillows at the end of the bed. She'd turned on the television, and Nick noticed it was an old movie he'd seen when he was a kid.

Uneasiness pricked at him, but he ignored it. He wasn't taking advantage of her. She needed ice for her foot, didn't she? And so what if he happened to pick her brain to satisfy his curiosity about a personal matter while he was lending aid. It was a classic quid pro quo arrangement. Nothing more than that.

"Hi," she said. "Thanks for the ice."

"Sure." He walked into the room, but saw the problem right away. Nothing to put the ice in. "Should I get a towel or something?"

She sat up and held out her hands for the bucket. He surrendered it.

"The plastic liner for the bucket will work." She deftly

picked up the bag, dumped the contents in the bucket, then palmed several handfuls of ice cubes and placed them in the bag.

"Would you like to sit down?" she asked as she worked.

Nick pulled a chair away from the small table and moved it toward the bed. He settled in it and watched her. She tied the bag closed and set the bucket on the nightstand. Leaning forward, she put the makeshift ice pack on her ankle. Admiration filled Nick at how efficient she was. Why should he expect different? If she were a doctor, she'd know exactly what was needed.

"I ordered some wine to be brought up. I figured it might take the edge off the pain."

She smiled at him, a secretive smile, as if she saw through his ploy. "Thank you for your help. I really appreciate it."

He glanced at the screen. "I love this movie. I haven't seen it in a long time."

She studied him. "Want to watch it?"

"Sure."

She turned up the sound. "It's one of my favorite movies."

"It had a cult following."

"I know. I was in that cult."

They watched it through to the end. Nick leaned back in the chair, reminiscing as he watched it. He'd made out with Andi Connors on the couch in her parents' living room while the movie had played on the television. And now he sat in a chair next to a woman on the bed in a hotel room actually watching the movie.

Damn, he was getting old. He was acting like the grandpa he had just found out he was. Bring on the hearing aids and medicine for erectile dysfunction. *Over the hill. Right here.*

"Can I ask you a question?"

Wariness replaced the amusement in her eyes. "Sure."

"I hope you don't mind. It's a medical question."

"Oh. All right."

"There's a…case I'm involved about a kid with leukemia."

Tomorrow turned her head and studied her foot. She leaned forward and repositioned the ice bag.

"What is the treatment for it?" Nick asked.

"Well, leukemia is a cancer that attacks the blood-forming cells. It starts in the bone marrow where blood cells are made. Chemotherapy would be the treatment plan, and depending on what kind of leukemia it is, the patient could get a transfusion of blood stem cells or even have bone marrow donated."

"Would the donor have to be a relative?"

"Not necessarily, but a relative would more likely be the best match." She looked at him then, and her expression looked almost fearful. "The donation of blood or marrow could save the patient's life."

"Do you think if one of the parents was on drugs, that would have caused their child to have it?"

Tomorrow lifted her hand and swiped at her eye, displacing her glasses and fixing them in a quick movement. "I don't think…." She shook her head. "Umm, I mean I could research it, but as far as I know parental drug use doesn't cause leukemia in their children."

"What if it was a genetic defect in one of the parents that caused the leukemia? Would a member of that person's family be obligated to donate?"

"You're talking ethically." She sighed. "Most cases of leukemia are not linked to any genetic factor so contributing a defective gene doesn't obligate a person ethically to become a donor. But I think we all are required to save a life if we have the capacity to do it. I mean if you could save the life of another person, why wouldn't you?"

"There would be a risk in donating."

"If it's just the blood stem cells, it would be no more risky than if you gave blood to the Red Cross. Donating bone marrow is maybe a little more so, but no more than, say, when you have a pin placed for a broken bone."

Nick ruminated on her words.

He was a grandfather.

He'd checked out the crazy story the woman had told him, and found that it appeared to be true. He wouldn't have believed her even enough to check out the story except for the pictures she'd sent him of her daughter.

The girl was the spitting image of Reg when he was little.

Nick still couldn't believe Reg would have gone to a sperm bank. It had to be because he'd needed money, and that was one way he could get it. And he would have had to have been clean at the time, or they wouldn't have taken the donation.

Right?

And even though he'd never met his grandchild, didn't her existence ethically bind him to provide a donation if it could save her life?

Nick sat back.

Did he believe in Tomorrow's approach to ethics? Save a life if you have the capacity to do it? But where did it end? If you believed that, you'd spend your whole life trying to help others. He couldn't even save his own son's life, though he'd had so many resources at his disposal. In the end, it wasn't enough. Reg had died anyway.

The stupid kid had thrown his life away for no damn good reason.

Nick clamped the thoughts down in his mind. He'd been through this a thousand times, and he thought he'd set it aside months ago. His whole life with Brenda and Reg seemed like a bad dream most days, and sometimes he could convince himself that was the case. In fact, he hadn't even thought about it lately.

Damn Reginald for doing one more stupid selfish thing to cause more havoc in Nick's life. And Damn Brenda for indulging him in every little thing until the day they both died in the wreck.

"Nick?"

Tomorrow's soft voice shook him out of his reverie. When he focused on her, he noticed she watched him with that assessing gaze she had, as if he were one of her patients, and she was checking him over to figure out what had brought him to her ER.

"What?"

"Someone is knocking."

Chapter Three

"Oh. Okay." Nick stood and walked across the room. He opened the door, took the tray of wine from the young woman in the telltale hotel blazer, and gave her a tip. She flashed a smile at his generosity. If he decided on a second bottle, he'd bet she'd get it here even faster.

He shut the door and brought the tray into the room, setting it on the table. "I ordered wine. I hope this is one of your occasions to drink it. Otherwise, I'll have to drink alone."

He noticed they'd included a cork screw, and he began the work of opening the bottle. He poured the wine and brought her one of the glasses.

She accepted it, holding it in front of her. "Should we make a toast?"

Nick sat down on the chair. "To Tomorrow, who I met today."

Her lips turned up in a smile. She clicked her glass to his. "I told you, I've heard it all before." She sipped the wine.

"Do you like it?"

"What? Your clever comments about my name?"

"I was referring to the wine, actually."

"Yes. Very nice."

"Good." Nick drank from his glass. It was very nice. "How's your foot? It's not broken, is it?"

She sipped more of the wine. "I don't think I will much care after a couple of glasses of this."

"So, what family business finds you at a hotel without a toothbrush?"

"I have a daughter."

Tomorrow's gaze penetrated his, as if that fact should

mean something to him.

He shrugged. "I have a granddaughter." It was the first time he'd acknowledged it aloud. It was strange to say it, and it didn't make it feel any more true, though he knew it was.

Tomorrow had begun coughing when he spoke, as if she had swallowed the wine wrong. Sitting up, she set the glass on the nightstand and covered her mouth with her hand. Nick waited unsure what to do. Finally, he stood and placed his knee on the bed, patting her on the back.

"You okay?" he asked, once the coughing had subsided.

She nodded, her attention on his shirt.

"I know it's shocking that I'm a grandfather. It sure shocked the hell out of me. Dammit, I thought I was too young for that."

"You must have had your son when you were very young." She leaned back, and when Nick took his hand away allowing her to move, she captured it and held it.

"I was nineteen. I thought my life was over, but Brenda and I got married, and...well...." He forced a smile, not wanting to open up that old wound. Instead, he clasped Tomorrow's fingers, thinking that he could do a lot worse than ending up in bed with her, if he were reading her signals right.

And even though he was a grandpa thanks to modern medicine and a sperm bank in Huntington, he sure as hell wasn't too old to know when a woman was coming onto him.

She recovered and took another drink. "But then you divorced?"

"Yes. Almost fourteen years ago now. What about you? How long have you been divorced?"

"I was never married."

Oh. She had a kid, but never bothered marrying the kid's dad. "That must be hard. Raising a child by yourself."

"It was my choice. She's my heart. I love her more than anything in this world."

"Yeah. Our kids are...." Nick sighed. "I...I had a son who died last year. He and my ex-wife were killed in a car wreck."

Tomorrow didn't say anything for a few minutes. Instead, she moved closer to the middle of the bed and tugged gently on his hand. The extra room allowed him to sit more comfortably on the mattress.

"If my daughter died, I don't think I'd want to live." Her hand tightened on his. "I'd want to die, too. I would do anything if it meant she could live."

His hip rested next to her body. Nick could feel her warmth, and the comfort of it tugged him like the tide to the moon.

"It must have been so difficult for you." Tomorrow gazed at him. He wondered what she looked like without her glasses.

"What doesn't kill you, makes you stronger, so they say."

"The bastards," she said vehemently. "They don't know."

He liked that spark of indignation. He wanted to know if he could taste it along with the wine on her lips. He moved forward a couple of inches and watched her reaction. Behind the lenses of her glasses, her pupils widened. Her lips parted.

He had his answer.

He leaned down and brushed his lips against hers. Her mouth was soft, pliant. She yielded to him, opening her mouth, and moving her tongue against his, and Nick growled in appreciation.

Tomorrow. Tonight, he was kissing Tomorrow.

He almost laughed at the silliness of the thought. Hold onto Tomorrow. Touch Tomorrow. Don't let go of Tomorrow. Make love until tomorrow with Tomorrow.

He gathered Tomorrow in with one hand, still holding her fingers with the other.

"Nick," she whispered petting the back of his head. "I want to make love to you."

"Okay." He nibbled on her neck, and she dropped her head back, like a cat enjoying a stretch. "Will you take your glasses off?"

She reached up with her hand, and he heard the frames fall against the nightstand, pinging the wine glass.

"I have to ask you something first."

"It's okay. I've got protection." He'd reached under her shirt and noted she was wearing a sports bra. He ran his fingers experimentally over the material and located her nipple. It beaded through the cloth.

"That's what I need to talk to you about. When's the last time you had a physical, and did they test you for venereal diseases?"

Nick burst out laughing and nipped her skin over her collarbone. "Is this how a doctor talks dirty?"

"Nick, I'm clean, and I want to be sure you're clean, too, because if you're not, we need to stop."

"Why?"

"Because I'm allergic to latex, and unless you have condoms made from sheepskin, then you can't use them."

He paused in his exploration of her skin and gazed at her. Without her glasses, he could see the color of her eyes more clearly. He'd thought they were blue, but blue didn't adequately describe the color. Summer sky blue. Caribbean ocean blue. A hue-a-man-could-get-lost-in-blue. Something nicked at his consciousness, but he ignored it, focusing instead on the bomb she just dropped on him. "You're kidding."

"No, so do you know?"

"Yes. I had a physical two months ago. You're a doctor. How can you be allergic to latex?"

"I use latex free gloves."

"What about birth control?"

"It's no longer an issue for me."

"So this is what it's like to make love to an older woman."

"Older woman?" Tomorrow slapped the back of his head. "How old are you?"

"Forty-four."

"When's your birthday?"

"February."

"Oh, good. You're two months older than I am."

"Whew. That was close. You were almost a cradle robber."

She dropped her head back, squeezing her eyes shut. "Oh, my gosh."

"What?"

"Nothing." She looked at him, smiling slightly then she leaned forward and kissed him.

Whatever ghost she'd wrestled with, she'd put it out of her mind. Or maybe she was having second thoughts about this?

"We don't have to do this, you know."

She shook her head in denial. "No take backs."

"Have you ever done this before?" He meant a one-night stand. This was what they were doing, right?

"Have you?"

"No." It was the truth, though from the way most of his colleagues had been acting all weekend, he was pretty sure he was in the minority.

She shimmied away from him, sat up, and took off her shirt, revealing a black sports bra encasing her breasts with cleavage that nearly set him to howling. Without pausing, she untied the drawstring at her waist and lifted her hips. He helped her move the pants down her legs and carefully lifted her calf of her injured foot. She was curvy, a swell to her hips and thighs which suited her large breasts. She lay back and watched him, reminding him of a figure from a Renaissance painting.

"Why don't you take off your bra?" he asked as he stood over her and unbuttoned his shirt.

"My breasts probably look better covered. They're forty-four years old, you know."

"Afraid I'll run from the room screaming?"

"A little."

"I won't."

The irises of her eyes darkened as she watched him shed

his shirt. He placed the shirt on the other bed and gripped his undershirt, pulling it off as well. Just to prolong the moment, he unclasped his watch and placed it next to her glasses, then slowly unbuckled his belt. Her attention was on his hands as he unzipped his pants. He wondered if the sound of metal against metal of the zipper was as arousing to her as it was to him.

He hated not to see what color her eyes turned when he was inside her, but he understood her reticence. "How about I turn out the lights, and you can take off your bra. And then there will be no danger of me being offended by your breasts." As if that could be an issue. He was dying to see them. Touch them. "Aren't you more comfortable with your bra off anyway?"

"You have no idea."

He grinned and walked across the room to hit the light switch, leaving the room illuminated by the glow of the television screen. Toeing off his shoes, he left them on the floor at the edge of the bed.

"Okay."

The television screen flickered blue light on Tomorrow, creating an alluring image as she pulled her bra over her head and tossed it aside on the bed. Nick stepped out of his pants and knelt beside her, resisting the urge to grab her flesh as if he were a fifteen-year-old virgin. He leaned into her and kissed her, melding their lips together. He lay beside her, careful to position her leg so that her foot still rested on the pillow. When her flesh grazed the bare skin of his chest, it nearly undid him, and he gripped her body, bringing her even closer, wanting her, needing everything she was offering him. He buried his face in her breasts and rained kisses on her, splaying his fingers around the ample globes and enjoying how damn soft she was.

When he brought his face toward her to meet her mouth again, he noted her lips were clamped shut.

"Tomorrow, sweetness, what's wrong? Why are you so tense? Do you want me to stop?"

"No. Please don't stop. I'm afraid I'm going to start moaning and making an idiot out of myself, and everybody in the hotel is going to know what we're doing."

"The walls are thick. No one's going to hear you except me."

"You know the breadth of hotel walls?" She said, suspicion evident in her tone.

He laved her in an attempt to distract her, but he noticed she was biting her lip now, and her body was as tense as a spring. He sat up and retrieved the remote from the other side of the bed and tilted it so he could see the buttons. Aiming it at the television, he hit the mute button and voices from the television filled the room.

The movie they both had enjoyed as teenagers had ended hours ago. So immersed they had been in their conversation, neither had noticed the detective show that played presently.

"Now then," he said. "If anyone hears moaning, they will assume it's the victim at the crime scene on TV." He threw the remote, and it landed close to where it had been. Nick claimed his place next to her. He brushed some hair away from her face that had escaped her ponytail. Her hair was curly, and he tugged at the curl and watched it spring back around his finger. "Okay?"

"All right."

He sealed his lips on hers, then moving to her neck, tasting her inch by inch. He felt her relax against him. He took his time exploring her, learning the landscape of her body until she guided him into her.

"Yes, Nick," she sighed against his mouth in that moment.

The sensation of no barriers between them overwhelmed him. He hadn't made love without a condom since he'd been married. It felt incredible. He was only aware of her velvet softness surrounding him, and the sweetness of her skin against his lips and hands. With surprise, he realized the guttural utterances of pleasure were coming from his own mouth. The world exploded, and he lay panting on top of her. For a moment, he couldn't move. But he felt her fingers on his back, drawing light circles on his skin.

I should move, but I don't want to.

Reluctantly, he lifted himself from her, missing her warmth as he did so. Her eyes were closed, and he realized he had forgotten to watch her while they made love, though with the dim light, he doubted he could have seen what hue of blue her eyes had turned.

He wanted to curl up next to her, tuck his face into those luscious breasts, and go to sleep, but already the ethereal quality of the lovemaking was dissipating, and his brain began to function again. He shifted and pulled the sheet over her.

"You're amazing," he whispered.

"Thanks, so are you." She blinked, and a tear rolled out of the corner of her eye.

Oh, shit. She was crying? Had he hurt her? He sat up and inspected her foot. The pillows and bag of ice were missing—probably knocked off the bed. He jumped up and began to fix it back.

"Don't. Just leave it. Really."

Her words stalled his attempt to fill the awkwardness of forgetting she was injured because he'd lost his mind making love to her. He stood there unsure what to do.

So, what happened now? Should he get her phone number? Would he call her even if he had it?

"It's okay if you want to go. I probably should get some sleep anyway," she said softly.

What? She wanted him to leave?

"Are you sure?"

She nodded and pulled the sheet closer to her chin.

"All right." He picked up his pants from the other bed and when he faced her again, her head was turned toward the window.

Dammit. He searched his mind for something to say, words to bridge the space widening between them by the second. He fought the urge to crawl back in bed with her and whisper apologies against her skin. Nothing seemed adequate enough to fix whatever he had done wrong. Hadn't she orgasmed? Shit, He didn't even know, he'd gotten so carried away. Obviously, she hadn't, and he hadn't cared enough to notice.

I'm sorry.

He almost said it, but wouldn't acknowledging it make it worse?

He grabbed his shirt and shoved his feet in his shoes, not bothering with his socks or undershirt, just fisted them and walked toward the door.

Can I call you? You can call me. Let's have breakfast. I'm a son of a bitch.

None of the words trampling across his mind left his lips. He opened the door, and pivoted to look at Tomorrow once more.

She'd turned her whole body away from him.

I am such a prick.

He opened the door and walked into the hallway. The door snicked shut behind him. He blew out a breath, wishing he could expel the regret of sleeping with a woman and leaving her without even knowing her last name.

He was too old to act this way.

Nick went back to his room, shrugging on his shirt as he walked up the flight of stairs. When he got back to his own room, he took a shower but it didn't wash off the self-recrimination. What had he been thinking? To pick up a woman in the stairwell and have sex with her. Tomorrow seemed so sweet, not like most women he knew who were out for a pound of flesh. She didn't strike him as the type to bed strangers. In fact, if he didn't know better, he would have thought she had little very little sexual experience. But she had a kid, and she was his age. Maybe she hadn't been with anyone since she had become a mom. If she worked full time and was a single parent, it didn't leave much room for anything else probably.

He was an idiot for leaving the way he did.

Nick finished his shower, dried off, and padded into the

bedroom. He pulled back the covers as he had seen Tomorrow do and lay down on the cool sheets. He stared at the ceiling. What was she doing right now? Had she gone to sleep? Was she still crying? Why had she been crying? Had he hurt her while they were lovemaking? It was her foot—had to be.

Or was it me?

He bunched the pillow under his head and turned on his side. He needed sleep. He was flying back in the morning. Maybe he could have breakfast with her before he left—make it up to her.

He deemed seven am was not too early to call her. If he was on the fence about inviting her out for breakfast, the fact that his watch was still in her room cinched it. He'd missed the timepiece when he had gotten dressed this morning and actually groaned out loud when he realized where it was. That damn watch had set him back 5000 dollars, and what does he do? Leaves it in the room of a woman he didn't even know her last name.

He had to get his watch.

When he dialed the room number, the woman who answered didn't sound much like Tomorrow.

"Hello? Is this Tomorrow?"

"No, it's today. Jason, is that you?"

Jason? For a second or two, Nick was at a loss for words. "It's Nick. I'm calling Tomorrow. This is her room, isn't it?"

"You're calling tomorrow? Why are you calling tomorrow? Who are you trying to reach?"

Nick huffed out a breath of frustration. The woman he was talking to obviously wasn't Tomorrow.

"Forget it." He hung up and sat down to put on his shoes. He must have dialed the wrong number. He'd just go down there and invite her to breakfast and get his watch back.

In a few minutes, he was at the door knocking. The door opened, and a woman who was definitely not Tomorrow stared at him.

"Umm, is Tomorrow here?"

She squinted at him. Her smeared make-up and lopsided hair testified that Nick's knock had awoken her.

"Huh?"

"I was in this room last night with a woman. Tomorrow. Is she in there?"

"You were in the room last night or tomorrow? What are you talking about?"

"I know it was this room," Nick snapped. "Are you alone?"

The door opened wider. Charlotte stood there, looking nearly as rung out as the other woman. "Nick? What are you doing here?"

What the hell?

The other woman looked at Charlotte. "He said he's coming back tomorrow."

"The conference is over today, Nick," Charlotte said. "Want to come in? Brittany can go somewhere else, can't you, Brittany?"

"Geez, Charlotte, you wake me up for this? I didn't get to sleep until almost four. I'm going back to bed."

"Is there another woman staying with you? A doctor. Her name is Tomorrow. I met her last night. This was her room."

Disappointment ran across Charlotte's face. "No, Nick. It's just me and Brittany." She stepped back and shut the door quietly.

Nick stared at the closed door and took a few deep breaths so he wouldn't beat the wood with his fist in frustration.

Dammit.

What happened to Tomorrow?

Chapter Four

"Are you pregnant?" Cole, the nurse, asked. "I'm sorry. I have to ask."

Tamara lay reclined on the examining table in ER 4. Her foot was so swollen, it had taken two people to get the shoe off. And the pain. She thought for a minute she would pass out.

"I know you do." I could be pregnant, but not likely. Even with such a slim chance, she knew to be cautious. "It's a possibility, and I want an apron just in case." Wearing a lead apron wasn't really necessary to have her foot X-rayed, but she didn't want to take any chances.

Cole's expression didn't give anything away. She'd finagled her way into his nursing care because she knew he didn't gossip. And even though it was a violation for staff to talk about a patient, which she was presently, things had a way of getting out.

She looked at him appealingly. "Who's the X-ray tech working today?"

"I'll see if Wendy's here."

Relief streamed through Tamara.

"We could do a pregnancy test while you're here."

Tamara shook her head. "It's too soon to be a positive."

He studied her face, and Tamara returned his gaze. Cole was a great guy. He nodded. "All right." He walked out of the room. "I'll be back in a few minutes."

Wendy arrived with the mobile X-ray machine not long after Cole left. She glanced at the window of the room, noting, Tamara was sure, that the blinds were closed. Then the tech picked up a lead apron on the cart and settled it carefully on Tamara's torso. In a moment, the picture had been taken, and Wendy wished her good luck.

Tamara lay back and stared at the ceiling. A small smiley face grinned down at her. How long has that been there? What a nice little detail for the patient to notice as they waited. Did all of the rooms have them?

She glanced at the clock, wondering if she had time to call home and talk to Miranda before Dr. Kenton arrived.

Her phone dinged, indicating she had a text.

What happened?

Tamara stared at the message from Charlotte.

Her foot throbbed, and had been since she'd walked across the airport before the sun came up this morning to catch her flight back.

Tamara texted back. *What do you mean?*

Big mistake, in a second, her cell rang.

"Nicolaus Pack was just here looking for you."

Fear shot across Tamara's mind, but years of staying calm in the midst of crisis allowed her to suppress it. "So? You didn't tell him anything, did you?"

"No. He was really freaked out. I thought you said he didn't know who you were."

"He didn't make the connection, no."

"You should have told him. You had the perfect opportunity."

"I think he's going to come around. I hope he will."

"You should have told him, or at least jumped him."

Dr. Shelly Kenton walked in the room, with Cole behind him.

"I have to go. I'll talk to you later." Tamara hung up her phone and held it next to her.

"Well, you were right. Fourth and fifth metatarsal fracture. Does this mean you're not coming in to work in 45 minutes?" Shelly said.

"I'm already at work. Put a boot on it."

Shelly grinned, his beard and moustache revealing all of his teeth reminding Tamara of a walrus. "I think I ought to contact the orthopedist on call. You might need surgery."

Tamara sat up and began to swing her legs over the side of the gurney. "I want to see the X-rays."

Cole stepped in front of her. "Come on, Tamara. It's not a good idea to be on that foot."

Tamara glared at him. She knew he was right, but she didn't like the nurse telling her what to do. "I'm going to be on it when my shift starts at 8."

Shelly stepped to the computer kiosk and began to type. "I don't know. Depends on if we can get you an orthopedic boot or not. Cole, I'm putting the order in. See what you can do because I do not want to stay over. I've been here since midnight, and I've got a date with my bed in 75 minutes."

Cole looked at Tamara and grinned. Shelly had been married two months, and his wife was gorgeous. Who could blame him for wanting to get home to her?

Shelly turned his head toward her. "How much pain are you in?"

"Not much. A two maybe."

The doctor pursed his lips. "As elevated as your blood pressure is? Now I know what your lying face looks like."

Her mistake had been walking through two airports and flying in a cramped airplane without elevating her foot. Not that she had had much choice. "Do you want the truth, or do you want to go home for your bed date?"

He shook his head and turned back to the screen. "I'll write you a prescription for—"

"I'll take some acetaminophen. I'm fine."

"Is that the woman's 'I'm fine'? Because that usually means the opposite."

"That's the medical doctor's 'I'm fine.'"

"Which also means the opposite," Cole supplied.

Both doctors looked at him, and he shrugged. "Am I wrong?"

No, he wasn't, but neither person told him so. "Why don't you go call about that boot?" Shelly said to Cole who glanced at Tamara before he walked out of the room. When the door shut behind him, Shelly turned to her. "I think it's a mistake to be on that foot today, Tamara."

"I'm not going home after I'm already here. I will manage."

"At least let me call Dr. Edisco in to look at it."

"It can't be that bad if you're ordering a boot."

He sighed. "Fourth and fifth metatarsals. Hairline fractures, but the edema is severe."

Tamara rubbed her face with her hands wearily. "Don't call Dr. Edisco. If I don't feel better with the boot and the acetaminophen, I'll call him."

"Lying face again."

"That is not professional patient rapport, Dr. Kenton."

"That's because I'm not dealing with a typical patient, Dr. Wallace. I'm dealing with one of my stubborn physician colleagues, but okay. I'm not answering my phone today if the hospital calls, so you just tell administration to call one of the other docs if you can't stick it out until four."

Tamara stared up at the smiley face and decided not to tell Dr. Kenton where he could stick it out until four.

****

Tamara clomped into the kitchen at half past four that afternoon. Her mother was at the stove stirring spaghetti sauce with a wooden spoon. Tamara could tell by the delicious aroma, and her mouth began to water.

Sandra did a double take at Tamara's leg encased in a big black air cast. With raised eyebrows, she commenced her stirring. "Atlanta was fun, huh?"

Tamara suppressed a shudder. "Not sure how to answer that, Mom." She approached the woman, kissed her cheek, and took the spoon from her. Dipping it in the sauce, she raised it to her lips and tasted it.

Delicious.

"Mmmm." Tamara stepped to the sink and washed the spoon and handed it to her mother. "Where's my sweet girl?"

"In the den watching television."

"How's she feeling?"

"Just fine."

"I'm going to get a shower real quick before I see her."
Miranda was a month into her chemo treatment, and Tamara
made it a habit to take a shower and change out of her work
clothes before she touched her daughter. With her immune
system, Tamara didn't like to take any chances.

She took the kitchen stairs to the second story and her
own bathroom, she sat on the side of the tub and carefully
removed the boot, then stripped the rest of her clothes
studying herself in the full length mirror briefly before
limping to the shower. Flashes of her and Nick naked in the
hotel room flew through her mind. Had that really been last
night? It almost seemed like a dream now, except her body
was tender in places. Wonderfully tender. The rasp of his
unshaven face against her breasts, the twinge at her thighs,
the unfamiliar sensations of lovemaking.

Because, really, Tamara hadn't made love before. Well,
except for that horrible disastrous time in college when she'd
almost died. She'd ended up in the emergency room, naked
and horrified—wishing really she would die, and scared that
she would. She and Aiden hadn't recovered from the incident
because the rubber condom he had been wearing was what
had caused her to go into anaphylaxis. He had stayed with her
in the hospital, but hadn't spoken to her after she had been
discharged.

Tamara wasn't bitter about it. In actuality, she was
thankful to Aiden because he could have just left her in her
dorm room, but instead he'd had the sense to call 911 and
had saved her life.

Last night had been scary—becoming intimate with a
man she'd just met and the fear of being discovered. But he
hadn't recognized her. Even when she'd taken her glasses off,
he hadn't known who she was.

He was beautiful, and he had willingly made love to her.

Plump, nerdy Tamara Wallace.

She smiled and leaned into the heat of the shower spray.
He'd lost himself in her. For a moment, she was as beautiful
and desirable as Charlotte.

The chance she was pregnant was slim—she knew that. They were both over 40, and one sexual encounter even with it being during a fertile time of her cycle, it was a long shot. But if she were, Miranda might have the donor she needed to live.

And maybe she wouldn't even need it. From the questions Nick had posed to her, she knew he was thinking about donating his own marrow.

And after last night, perhaps she had a little more leverage. She could call him, bring him his watch, ask for him to be tested.

Would he agree?

Tamara finished her shower, towel-dried her hair, and dressed. In a few moments, she descended the staircase to cartoon noises.

Miranda lay on the couch with her blankie tucked next to her, and Gary the cat at a respectable distance on the next cushion.

"Hi, Miranda. How's my girl this afternoon?" Tamara leaned down and kissed her daughter then picked her up and sat on the couch, settling her on her lap.

"Mama!" Her small arms wrapped around Tamara, and she squeezed. "I really missed you."

"I'm sorry, sweetie. I had to go on a trip to meet Charlotte."

"Our Chocolate?" Miranda's nickname for Charlotte.

"Yes."

"How come I couldn't go?"

"It wasn't a kid kind of trip. What did you do while I was gone?"

Miranda's skin had a good pallor to it. Her eyes seemed bright, normal. Relief and anxiety battled with each other, a common response any time Tamara saw her daughter these days. Tamara kissed the top of her head and ran her fingers along the baby-soft hair. A tuft of hair followed the movement of her hand, leaving Miranda's scalp, and fear exploded in Tamara's chest.

"What, Mama?"

Stop it. You knew this was going to happen.

"Nothing, sweetie." Tamara gripped the hair in her fingers. "It's so good to see you. Did you eat ice cream last night?"

"Yep."

Tamara's throat closed, and she attempted to swallow the lump. "Let me guess. Rainbow sherbet."

The little girl grinned. "Yep."

Tamara ran her hand lightly over Miranda's head again. More hair.

"Have you been hurting anywhere?"

She tucked her thumb in her mouth and shrugged. That was a yes.

"Did you tell Meemee?"

Miranda turned and began to watch television. That was a no.

Frustration rose in Tamara. She didn't want her daughter to be in pain, but Miranda didn't like taking medicine at all. Soon, she'd become used to it, but for now, each dose was a battle, and the two times she'd had the chemo had been like dealing with a demon child.

"Point to where it hurts."

Without looking away from the screen, Miranda pointed to her hip and her shoulder.

Tamara touched the ridge of her spine through her shirt. "What about here?"

She shook her head.

"Did Gary eat any of your sherbet?"

She shook her head again.

"I'm thinking sherbet sounds good. Want some?"

Miranda's face turned to her mom. Finally. "Meemee says no ice cream before supper," she said around her thumb.

"Yeah, but I'm the mom."

Her teeth appeared around her hand in a grin. "It'll spoil supper."

"Maybe one bite?"

"Maybe."

"With a pill?"

"Two bites, and a Sprite."

"Pill first."

Miranda shook her head.

"Guess I'll have to eat the two bites then."

"You'd do that to your baby?"

Tamara laughed and hugged her. "I don't want my baby to hurt."

"The med'cine makes me hurt."

"The med'cine's hurting the bad stuff inside you. The pill will help the pain, Miranda."

"No."

"How about a sherbet float?"

"Nope. Nope. Nope."

"Tamara?" Sandra called. "Your phone's ringing." She brought Tamara's phone in the room and handed it to her.

Tamara looked at the screen briefly.

Pack Bryan and Levine

Nick was calling her.

Tamara took a deep breath, swiped her phone screen, and held the phone to her ear.

"Hello?"

"Ms. Wallace? This is Nicolaus Pack. I'd like to meet with you."

Thump. Thump. Thump.

"Mama. Mama." Miranda tugged at her arm.

"When?" Tamara asked, patting Miranda's hand, hoping it would assuage her.

"Tomorrow at nine o'clock."

"Mama. Maamaaaa...."

"Can we do it later in the day? I have to work tomorrow." Tamara held her daughter's hand and brought it to her lips to kiss it.

"I thought you wanted to meet with me."

"I do."

"Maamaa. Mommy!"

"Then tomorrow at nine is what I have available. Do you want the appointment?"

Tamara shifted the little girl on her lap. Several strands of hair strayed onto her sleeve and separated from Miranda's head. Tamara looked at those hairs clinging to her clothing. "Yes. Yes, I want the appointment."

"See you then."

Tamara heard a click, then nothing. She lowered the phone and saw the call information disappear. He'd hung up.

If she hadn't seen him with her own eyes, heard him, felt him, no one could have convinced her the man in the hotel room last night was the same jerk she'd just spoken to on the phone.

She focused on her daughter still pulling on her hand.

"What is it, sweetheart?"

"I wanna a sherbbie throat."

"A sherbet float?"

"Yes."

"With a pill."

"Sherbbie throat now. Then a pill."

Tamara looked at her mother who was standing in the doorway of the kitchen. She shrugged. "If she was really hurting, she'd take the pill."

"I'm not sure she would. I'm beginning to figure out where the stubbornness comes from."

"Really?" Sandra asked.

"What's stop-burn-ness?" Miranda asked, her suspicious expression made Tamara wonder if she thought they were talking about more pills.

"Who was on the phone?" Sandra said.

"The stubborn side of the family. He wants to meet with me tomorrow, and too bad that I'm working. I guess all the traumas and sickness in the county can step aside to accommodate his schedule."

"I could meet with him," the older woman offered.

Tamara shook her head. "Oh, Mom. I think I better do it. This trip I took to Atlanta probably complicated things."

"So, you did get to meet with him."
"Yes."
Oh, boy, had she.

Chapter Five

Déjà vu.

Tamara sat in the same chair she'd occupied the last time she'd been here. But she hadn't bothered with straightening her hair or putting in the contacts.

Why bother?

He'd seen her naked. Trying to pretty herself up wouldn't make a difference at this point. In fact, him seeing her naked was only going to make this meeting more uncomfortable. More awkward.

More difficult.

Tamara had run through every scenario of how today would go, hoping it would prepare her for his reaction, whatever it was going to be.

The phone rang, and Jessica Adams, administrative assistant, answered it. She paused and answered, "Yes, sir." She hung up and stood. Walking across the room and standing at the door, she looked back at Tamara and nodded.

Tamara gripped the arm rest and stood. With the boot on, she walked as gracefully as she could toward whatever was going to happen next.

Jessica knocked then opened the door.

"Tamara Wallace is here," she announced, once again getting the pronunciation wrong.

Tamara walked into the doorway. "It's pronounced Tamara, like tomorrow. Thank you."

Nick stood behind his desk in a suit. Another man stood in front of the desk, but Tamara's attention riveted to Nick. He studied her face for a full minute, then his gaze wandered down to her body, snagging on the orthopedic boot.

Desire exploded in Tamara. Images of two nights ago

played through her brain. She didn't want to think of that right now, of him kissing her, worshipping her body, whispering how beautiful and soft she was.

His expression gave nothing away, but she saw a muscle twitch at his jaw.

Oh, Lord, help me do whatever it takes to save Miranda.

"Ms. Wallace?" a voice said. The other man, though Tamara still watched Nick who hadn't moved.

Tamara tore her gaze away from him and saw the other man standing next to her with his hand outstretched. "I'm John Levine. How do you do?"

"It's Dr. Wallace. I am well, thank you."

"You're a doctor? Of what, may I ask?"

"Medical Doctor. I work in the emergency department at Acorn County Hospital in Arms Fork."

Nick crossed his arms over his chest. "Easy access to medical equipment like air casts. Is that to illicit sympathy?"

"The boot is to ambulate the foot which sustained two fractures two nights ago. I can have the X-rays sent to you, if you like."

"Very convenient, the fall. It engendered an escort to your hotel room," Nick snapped.

"Have you two met?" John asked. "Nick, I thought you said—"

"Oh, we've met. We are *very* well acquainted, even though I was not aware of it until now. Would you concur, Tamara?"

Tamara glanced behind her. The administrative assistant was gone and the door shut, thankfully.

Tamara approached his desk. "Nick, can we talk alone?"

"I'm afraid not," John said.

Nick's perfect mouth turned up in an evil smile. "You do your best talking alone with me, is that it?"

She probably deserved that, so she didn't try to defend herself, just waited for the next jab.

His predatory gaze moved over her once again. "Yes. I would like to talk to you alone."

"No, Nick. Bad idea. As your lawyer, I'm advising you against it."

"Two minutes," Nick said between gritted teeth.

John shook his head. "No."

"Get out, John, dammit."

John sighed. "I will step outside for two minutes." He walked over to the door, opened it, and walked out, leaving the door ajar. Nick strode over to the door and slammed it shut.

He glared at Tamara. "So, you're going to blackmail me. If I don't give your daughter what she needs, you'll go to the media, is that it?"

"No, Nick. I swear, I'd never do anything like that. I don't want anyone to know what happened between us the other night. I have a daughter to think about."

He stalked toward her until they were almost touching. Tamara stood her ground and tilted her face to keep eye contact.

"I hope you don't expect me to believe the other night was a coincidence."

"No, I don't expect you to believe that."

"How long have you been stalking me?"

"I found out you were at the conference and flew down there hoping I could—"

"Entrapment."

"I just wanted to talk to you, to try to convince you—"

He barked out a laugh of derision and stepped away from her, turning his back. "Convince me? Dammit, I didn't know how gullible I could be. Here I thought all of the sharks were the lawyers at the conference. And I escort the most bloodthirsty one to her room and order wine!" He banged his fist on his desktop.

"If I had told you who I was, would you have listened to me? I waited out there two hours with an appointment, and you wouldn't talk to me. I stood in the hallway and told you your granddaughter—"

"Don't you call her that. I don't have any

grandchildren."

"All right. All right. I told you my daughter had leukemia, and you wouldn't give me five of your minutes. You didn't even see me. If you had, you would have recognized me in Atlanta."

"I am a very busy person."

"I know that, Nick, but my daughter could die. I don't care what you think about me. I don't care what you call me. I don't care what you do to me, but, please, for her sake, take a blood test to see if you can give her the marrow she needs to save her life. She means everything to me. I don't want her to die."

The door had opened and closed during Tamara's speech. She didn't have to look behind her to know John Levine had walked back in the office. Instead she watched Nick, his back still to her.

"I will do whatever it takes to save her life. I will do whatever you want me to, but please help her. Don't punish her because I did something stupid the other night."

He walked around his desk and opened a drawer. He looked into it, studying whatever was there.

"I want to meet her."

"Nick," John said approaching him and indicating a typed-document on the desk. "Have Dr. Wallace sign this, and let's keep this as impersonal as possible."

Relief blanketed Tamara. Yes, she liked John Levine's advice.

"What is it?" she asked.

"It states that Nick will agree to a blood test and, if appropriate, a donation of stem cells or marrow, but you are not to contact him except through me, and you agree that he is not financially responsible for Miranda Wallace in any manner, including medical expenses."

All of those stipulations seemed reasonable. "All right."

"Your lawyer should look that over before you sign it," Nick said, shutting the drawer and sitting down on the chair behind the desk. "And I want to meet her. Today."

No! She didn't want Nick to be part of Miranda's life. Tamara glanced at John, hoping he would intervene.

"Nick," John said. The two men stared at each other. A message passed between them, and Tamara held her breath hoping Nick would see reason. John shook his head, but Nick continued to watch his legal counsel.

John shrugged and picked up the paper. "Are you sure?"

Fear chilled Tamara, and she rubbed her arms. John had lost the battle of wills.

"Do you want me to add it in?" he asked.

Nick turned his gaze on Tamara. Once again, he assessed her from head to toe. "Yes. I am allowed visitation if I give Tamara 24 hours' notice."

"What if it's not convenient for me?"

Nick watched her. It was uncanny how similar his and Miranda's eyes were. "I'm a reasonable person."

"I don't think it's a good idea for you to—"

"You said you'd do anything as long as I have the test and give her the marrow if I can. Did you mean it?"

"Yes, I meant it, but she's only four. This is a very vulnerable time for her, and if she gets upset, it could further compromise her immune system."

"What's wrong with her immune system?"

"She's taking chemotherapy. It weakens everything—the cancer, but the good cells as well. Her immunity is very low right now. That's why we're keeping her home."

"Who's we?"

"My... mother lives with me. She keeps Miranda when I'm working. If you insist on seeing her, it will confuse her. She's not going to understand who you are. What you are."

"Tell her I'm a friend."

"I don't bring friends home."

"Boyfriends, you mean." Nick's gaze burned into Tamara.

She didn't respond. She'd told Nick she didn't care what he thought of her, and she meant it.

"Okay, but promise me, you won't disrupt her life. Her

health has to be the most important thing. You won't try to get custody of her, and you won't try to impose visitation after the procedure is complete." Tamara looked at John. "Can you put that in the document? That he relinquishes any parental rights he has regarding my child."

"I might want to see her after the procedure. Would you deny me that if I can save her life?"

"You said you didn't have any grandchildren."

He waved his hand in a dismissive gesture. "I'm sorry I wasted your time."

He was bluffing, she was pretty sure. Could she call his bluff? "When I saw you in the hallway a few weeks ago, I knew who you were because Miranda has your eyes. The same beautiful green."

They kept eye contact until Tamara swore the tension popped sparks between them. She reached into her bag and retrieved his watch she had placed in the inside pocket. Gathering it in her fist, she continued to hold his gaze as she set it on the edge of his desk. That green-fire gaze broke as he studied the object she'd placed in his vision. He swiveled his chair toward the computer screen and began to type.

"I won't attempt to gain custody or impose visitation rights regarding Miranda Wallace."

"I don't want her name in the document."

"Fine. The daughter of Tamara Wallace."

"No. I don't want it even that specific. I don't want her ever to know we had to do this because of her."

"The child of Tamara Wallace then." He jabbed at the backspace key and began to type again.

The printer hummed to life, and Nick stood up and picked up the paper out of the tray. "Have your attorney read that over. If there aren't any other issues, have it signed in the presence of a notary."

He handed it to her, and Tamara took it from him and sat down. She read it carefully.

After her second time through the document, she looked up at Nick then at John, both of whom were seated and silent as she read. "I'll sign this. Is either of you a notary?"

Nick picked up his phone. "Jessica? Would you come in here please?"

****

Tamara drove from Nick's office straight to the hospital and worked the rest of her shift. She noticed Nick sent her a text at four asking to meet Miranda tonight.

So much for 24 hours' notice.

She didn't reply to his text, nor the next one which came an hour later. Because Shelly had covered for her this morning, she stayed later and worked three of his hours, putting her getting home after seven.

Miranda's high-pitched screaming met Tamara as soon as she opened the door from the garage. She dropped her bag and ran as best she could in the boot toward her daughter.

She followed the sounds to Miranda's bedroom where the little girl stood on her bed, large patches of her scalp visible now and her mouth open as she wailed. Sandy sat on the edge of the bed.

"Is it...?" Tamara couldn't bring herself to say the word hair. Of course, that was what this was about. Miranda had never had her hair cut her entire life. She loved her long blonde hair.

Tamara's mother held up a brush that had little girl hair hanging from the bristles. "It's coming out in clumps."

"Why are you brushing it?"

"I wasn't. She was."

Tamara reached for her daughter, but she ran to the far corner of the bed. "No. Don't get me."

"Honey, it's all right. It's just the medicine making your hair come out. It will grow back."

"I hate the medicine. I hate it!" She hit her head on the wall, and Miranda climbed on the bed and scooped her daughter into her arms.

"Stop it. Stop." She sat down on the bed attempting to cradle her daughter in her arms. Miranda continued to cry, already a whelp forming on her forehead where she'd connected to the wall. Tamara tried to hold her, Miranda wouldn't have it. She screamed and flailed her arms and legs. Tamara placed her in a bear hold and waited for her to calm down.

"No, Mommy, No!"

"Calm down, Miranda."

"Let me go!"

The child bit down on Tamara's hand, and in shock, she released her grip. Miranda slid to the floor and ran out of the bedroom, and into the bathroom. The door slammed.

Sandra came into the room. "Nicolaus Pack is here."

Tamara hadn't even heard the doorbell. It didn't matter. She didn't have time to deal with Nick right now. "Why didn't you catch her?"

"She's already upset enough. Me trying to hold her down will make it worse. Did you hear what I said?"

"Tell him now is not a good time."

"I did."

"Please tell me you didn't let him in the house."

"I didn't, but he's on the porch waiting."

Tamara sighed. She marched to the door and opened it. Nick's angry gaze met hers.

"This isn't a good time, Nick."

"It's as good as any." He stepped forward, probably thinking she was going to move out of his way.

"Look. My daughter is having a meltdown right now because her hair is falling out of her head by the handful." She held up a lock of hair, and his gaze locked on it. "So, unless you can fix this—which you can't—then you are not coming in the house, you are not meeting her, you are not visiting today. Go away, and I'll call you later."

Tamara slammed the door and went back to the bathroom door. Fortunately, the knob had a hole in which the lock could be popped with a small screwdriver.

"Why don't you just leave her in there and let her calm herself down?" Sandra said.

"Because she's four years old, and there are things in

there she can hurt herself with."

"Like what? Your whole house is childproofed."

"She knows how to get the cabinets open. Those locks just slow her down for a little while."

Tamara fetched the screwdriver and unlocked the door. Miranda had curled up in a ball in between the toilet and the bathtub.

Oh, baby. I wish I could make this easier for you.

"Leave me 'lone!"

"I will, but you need to go in your room first."

"No!"

"You can go in my room, Mommy's room, or your room. Which one do you want to go in?" Sandy asked.

"Your room, Meemee."

"All right."

Tamara crossed her arms over her chest and watched her daughter crawl to Sandy who reached her arms down and picked the girl up.

"Your room," Miranda said.

Tamara backed up and watched her mother carry her daughter down the hall, then she heard her mother's footsteps down the stairs to the mother-in-law suite where Sandy's bedroom was. Tamara shouldn't be angry that her mother had intervened. The woman, perhaps, had deescalated the situation, but Tamara didn't have to like it. Miranda was only four. She couldn't understand that the medicine which was making her hair fall out was the same medicine which was saving her life. How could Tamara help her to see that?

She checked on Miranda after a while, and though she had calmed down, she was still crying softly, her thumb pushed in her mouth. When Tamara came in the room, her daughter shook her head.

"Go away, Mommy."

Sandy watched Tamara steadily as she held Miranda to her.

She's my daughter. I should be the one to comfort her.

Tamara pivoted on her booted foot and went back

upstairs. She cleaned the kitchen and did a load of clothes. Her phone signaled she had a text, and when she looked at the screen, she saw it was from Nicolaus Pack.

Can't he take a hint already?

This is Nick. Three bags on your door step.

What did that mean?

Tamara went to the front door and opened it. Three shopping bags sat on the front porch. She looked around, but didn't see Nick. Had he just deposited the bags and left? What was in them?

She bent down and opened one.

She gasped in pleasure and reaching into the bag, she pulled out a cap with the logo of Miranda's favorite movie on it. Two long locks of braided hair trailed from either side of the cap to look like the heroine from the movie. Two more caps just like it rested in the bag. The other bag from a fandom novelty store in the mall had a rainbow colored clown wig, a yellow, green, and black Jamaican knit cap with dreadlocks, and a pirate hat and bandana. The third bag was from a girly store Miranda loved to frequent. From the contents, it seemed Nick had bought one of every hat and scarf in the store.

Hmm.

Was it a bribe to meet Miranda?

If so, it might work.

Tamara placed the braided cap on her head tucking her hair inside of it and carried the bags downstairs.

Miranda quieted when she saw her mother in the doorway.

"Do you like my hat?" Tamara asked.

"Oh, my. What stylish hair, Tamara," Sandy asked.

"I think so, and look, there's one for each of us." Tamara pulled out the other braid hats. "Meemee, do you want one?"

"Yes. Thank you." Sandy took the cap and put it over her hair.

"What about you, Miranda?" Tamara held out the hat

and waited.

Miranda reached her hand forward. Tamara laid it in her tiny fingers and watched the fingers curl over the ice blue braids, feeling the artificial hair. Then she settled it in her lap, petting it with the non-thumb sucking hand as if it were Gary, their cat.

"Want to see the other hats?"

She shook her head 'No'.

"Would you like me to show you?"

She gave an affirmative nod.

Tamara sat on the foot of the bed and pulled out each wig, hat, and scarf. She and Sandy discussed each one as Tamara held it out for Miranda's inspection. By the time the bags were emptied, Miranda's mood had improved and she even ate a snack of apple sauce before going to sleep.

Tamara texted Nick with a short message thanking him. Within seconds her cell phone rang.

She sighed in resignation and answered it.

"Hello," Nick responded to her greeting.

Tamara didn't speak. She'd already thanked him. Why was he calling her?

"Are you there?" he asked.

"Yes."

"Did the hats and hair help?"

"I think so."

"Good."

Silence stretched between them.

"You're not going to make this easy, are you?" he finally said.

"Nothing is easy right now."

"I want to meet her."

"I know."

"When?"

"She's asleep."

"So, not tonight. Tomorrow night? I can be there by seven."

"Seven isn't going to work. That's her bath time, then

she's in bed by seven-thirty."

"I'm trying to be very patient about this. You've invited me into this situation. I do not think I'm being unreasonable by wanting to see her."

Tamara didn't like how Nick wanted to call the shots in seeing Miranda. She knew his kind. There were many doctors like him at the hospital. They were controlling and demanding. They thought they knew the best thing to do in every situation, but they didn't. Tamara was not going to let him control this situation. If he ever did meet Miranda, it would be because Tamara wanted it to happen.

"I invited you into this situation because I need a donor match for my daughter. She doesn't need a grandfather. She already has a family."

For a long moment, Nick didn't speak, and then, "I understand."

"I will contact your lawyer about the test. Goodbye, Nick."

Chapter Six

Nick and John sat at the table in the conference room. It was nearly eight in the evening, but with all of the time Nick had put into Tamara Wallace yesterday, he was behind. And he still couldn't get his damn mind on his work.

"Can you read this?" John handed him a handwritten deed, an original, Nick was sure.

Nick held the document in front of him. "I'm giving her exactly what she wants. Why won't she let me see that kid?"

John sighed. "Would you put Tamara Wallace out of your mind and focus?"

Nick looked at the paper. He read it aloud. "There. You happy? Now help me figure out how I'm going to get in her house."

"Give her 24 hours' notice."

"I did. She said Miranda was too tired from a doctor visit." He scrolled through the sixty page deposition he'd been working on.

"Seems like if Miranda is sick, her mom will probably do whatever she wants."

Her mom sure as hell would do whatever it took to get *his* cooperation, including having sex with him. My God, the danger she put herself in. If he had been the kind of man to beat a woman up, she could have been hurt.

Images of them together flashed through his brain.

"Yeah, so?"

"So, you sent the hats and wigs. That was a great idea. Send something else. Order her a Super Cooper wig with a tiara on it."

"A what?"

"Lily's six. It's her favorite show." Lily was John's daughter. "Super Cooper is a super hero girl. She rescues animals and occasionally people. She has this frosty blue green hair and a tiara. It's hideous. You find a Super Cooper wig and a tiara, I bet you'd get to meet little Miranda."

"Super Cooper, huh?"

"Yeah. And she wears a diamond encrusted cape, too."

Nick minimized the document on his laptop and opened up the Internet icon.

****

"Mama, when's that man getting here?" Miranda asked.

Tamara stood at the china cabinet trying to decide if *that man* deserved Mom's fine china. She looked down at her daughter, a little hard to recognize under her Super Cooper hair.

Tamara had to give it to Nicolaus Pack. When the super hero hair, tiara, and cape had arrived Fed-ex, Miranda had been ecstatic. The wig had been altered—a soft lining had been placed on the inside of the cap so that it didn't irritate Miranda's sensitive scalp. The marking on the material identified the origins from a company specializing in products for cancer patients. Tamara had researched the site but found no Super Cooper wigs there. She surmised Nick had bought the items separate and had someone affix the cap to the wig so Miranda could wear it comfortably.

That extra effort had shocked her, but it had touched her as well.

So, when Miranda had asked who had given her the Super Cooper dress up things, Tamara had answered honestly.

"His name is Nicolaus Pack, and he's your grandfather."

"What's a grandfather?"

Tamara sighed. How to explain it? Her mother had interjected.

"He's part of your family. But distant. You've never met him," Sandy said.

That seemed to satisfy Miranda, but then later that evening at bedtime. She'd asked about Nick again.

"Mama, why did that man give me my Super Cooper hair?"

Because he wants to get his way.

Tamara tucked the blanket around her daughter. "He thought you'd like it."

"How does he know me?"

"I told him about you. I think you're pretty special, and I wanted him to know, too."

"Can he come here and see me being Super Cooper?"

"I don't know."

"I want him to see me."

Tamara leaned forward and kissed her daughter. "Goodnight, Sweetie. I love you." She reached for the wig.

"No." Miranda held it to her head. "I want to keep it on."

"No. It's not good for you to sleep in it. It will inhibit your skin from—"

"Tamara," Sandy said.

Tamara looked at her mother.

"I'm sure after Miranda goes to sleep, you can settle things." She raised her eyebrows meaningfully.

Oh.

So, the wig stayed on which saved Tamara from having to be the bad guy and Miranda from getting upset. In the living room a few minutes later, Sandy had taken Miranda's side as well about Nick.

"What would it hurt to let him meet Miranda?"

"Mom, he's heartless. Ruthless."

"He can't be heartless. Look what he's already done for her."

"He's only plying her with gifts because he thinks I'll give in."

"He's her grandfather."

"No, Mom. He's the father of a sperm donor."

"Biologically, he is her grandfather. He may be able to save her life. Let him meet her."

Tamara had picked up her cell and texted him with a brief message: *Dinner at my house to meet Miranda tomorrow 6pm.*

His responding text came back an hour later.

I accept.

The doorbell rang. Tamara looked at the clock on the wall. He was twenty minutes early. Miranda's eyes went wide.

"That man's here." She skipped to the front door.

"Wait," Tamara said. "Not yet." Tamara wanted him to wait on the stoop for a few minutes as a payback for the two hours he had made her wait. But already Miranda was opening the door.

Tamara followed and saw her daughter standing there staring up. When Tamara arrived at the door, she saw that Miranda was looking at Nick, dressed in his standard suit and tie.

He must have greeted her already because Miranda said, "No, I'm not. I'm Super Cooper. Can't you tell?"

He blinked a few times. Anxiety rose in Tamara's chest. He'd better not be hateful to her little girl.

"I thought Miranda Wallace lived here." He held out a bouquet of flowers. "I brought these for her."

Miranda brought her hands up to her mouth. "You did? For me?"

"Do you like flowers?"

Miranda reached up and took the bouquet. She pivoted and ran toward the kitchen. "Meemee, Meemee!"

Nick had been leaning down toward Miranda. He straightened and gazed at Tamara. Her heart had already been racing when she'd seen him standing at the door, but when that emerald gaze connected with hers, her heart sped even more.

The easy manner he'd shown to her daughter fell off him as if he had shed a coat. They stared at each other for a moment.

Please say you can't stay. That something came up.

"Are you going to invite me in?"

"You've met her. Wasn't that what you wanted?"

"Your text said dinner."

Tamara tried to think of something witty and biting that would discourage him from wanting to eat dinner with them.

Charlotte would know what to say.

"Hello," Sandy said from behind Tamara. "Of course, we want you to have dinner with us." She patted Tamara. "Don't we, Tamara?"

"Hey, Look." Miranda appeared in between them and held up a vase. "Meemee gave me this to put the flowers in. Come on." She left again, heading further into the house.

Nick stepped into the foyer and held out his hand to Tamara's mother. "Hello. I'm Nicolaus Pack."

"I'm Sandy Wallace, Tamara's mother." She accepted Nick's hand and shook it.

"It's very nice to meet you, Mrs. Wallace."

"Please call me Sandy."

"Come on, people!" Miranda said.

Plates clattered against each other, alerting Tamara that Miranda had decided to set the table herself. Tamara followed the noise to the dining room and saw her putting salad plates where the dinner dishes should be.

"No, honey. These are for salad." Tamara reached into the cabinet and picked up the larger plates. "This is what we need."

"Can't we use the little plates too?"

"We're not having salad."

"I want a little plate. That man wants one too."

"You can't know what he wants because you haven't asked him."

Miranda turned toward the door to where Nick and Sandy had entered. "Don't you want a little plate?"

"Yes, I do," Nick replied.

"See? I told you."

Anger bubbled under Tamara's skin. She placed the dinner plates on the table, removed one and stacked a salad plate on top of it. "Why don't we do this? Salad on top. Dinner on the bottom. Then later when you don't want your food touching each other, we will have a bigger plate to spread out on."

The little girl looked at the plates. "Oooh, Mommy, I

love that idea."

Tamara smiled down at her daughter. "I thought you might."

"Everything is ready," Sandy said. "Tamara and I can get the food out of the kitchen."

Tamara didn't want to leave Nick alone with her daughter. Miranda laid another dinner plate on the table and placed a salad plate on top. "That man and me can get the plates on the table."

"Honey, don't call him that man," Sandy counseled on her way out of the room.

Uh-oh. What should she call him then?

Nick watched the little girl. Did he think she looked like his son?

"What are you?" Miranda asked him. "Meemee told me, but I forgot."

"He's related to you biologically, Miranda," Tamara said.

"Yeah, but what's the word?"

"You can call him Mr. Pack." Tamara set the rest of the dishes on the table, hoping Nick would say something, give some indication of what he would like to be called.

"That wasn't it."

"That's his name."

"Huh." She marched up to Nick. "BRB. You know what that means?"

"No."

"It means be right back."

"Where are you going?" Tamara asked.

"The kitchen. BRB, Mommy." She put her hands on her hips and marched out of the room.

Tamara's gaze followed her daughter out of the room.

"She can call me Nick."

"Why didn't you say so?"

"I didn't know what you've told her."

"The truth is a little hard for her to understand at this point." Tamara put the plates around the table.

"Has she ever asked about her father?"

"No."

"What will you tell her when she does ask?"

"I will tell her that she had a biological father who is no longer living." Tamara decided to leave the salad plates for Miranda to place. She moved the vase of flowers to the middle of the table.

The kitchen door swung open hitting the wall. Little girl footsteps approached. "Meemee said you're my grandfarther. Grand. Farther. Grandfarther."

Tamara resisted the urge to sigh her frustration.

Sandy stepped into the room with hot pads on her hands holding a casserole dish. "Put a trivet there, would you?"

Tamara opened the drawer of the sideboard and pulled one out and laid it near the vase.

"Grandfarther. Grandfarther."

"Grandfather," Sandy corrected. "Grand means big. And Father, like mother and father."

Tamara left the room thinking she could use the excuse of getting the asparagus, but wanting to get away from the discussion. She didn't want Miranda to know about a grandfather, especially not a grandfather who was Nicolaus Pack. He had said he didn't have any grandchildren. She'd had to beg him to help save Miranda's life. He would never be a grandfather to her. Why would her mother do this? Hadn't Tamara made it clear to her that the only role Nick had in Miranda's life was as a donor?

A lot like the role that Nick's son had in Miranda's life. As a donor only. Anything else would be too messy.

He didn't want to be her grandfather.

And Tamara didn't want him to be. She just wanted a donor for her child.

That was it.

God, get me through this night. Let him be a match. But most of all, please let her live.

Tamara picked up the serving platter and the basket of rolls. Taking a few deep breaths, she pushed through the door. Mom stood at the sideboard pouring water in glasses from a crystal pitcher. Miranda and Nick were already sitting at the table next to each other. Nick was in Mom's chair. Obviously, she had been relocated to the other side of the table. At least, Nick wasn't directly across from Tamara. Not that it mattered that much. Any place at the table was going to be too close.

Tamara made one more trip to the kitchen to retrieve the pear salad, a favorite of Miranda's. Mom had sat down by the time Tamara returned, so she took her own place at the table.

"We hold hands when we pray, Nicky," Miranda stated.

"Nicky?"

"Grandfather was a bit of a mouthful," Sandy said.

"Apparently, Nick was too short." He grasped the hands which Sandy and Miranda offered to him.

"And it goes like ee on the end like Meemee's name. Nick-ee. Meemee. See that, Mommy?"

"Yes, I see. Are you going to pray for us, Miranda?"

Tamara bowed her head, but she watched Miranda, who closed her eyes. And Tamara watched Nick, who also watched Miranda.

"God is great. God is good. Let us thank him for our food. By His hands, we are fed. Thank you, Lord, for daily bread. Amen."

During the prayer, his intense gaze bore into Tamara's. She was the first one to break away, looking once again to her daughter.

Afterward, the little girl looked at her grandfather. "It's not just for bread. The prayer's for all the food. We just say bread cause that's how the prayer goes."

"It would be hard to find a word to rhyme with asparagus." Sandy stood up and doled portions of chicken and rice casserole on each person's plate.

"I'm not thankful for sparagus, Meemee."

"Nevertheless, you can try a bite," Tamara told her daughter and placed a single spear on her plate.

"I already tried it before, and it is gross and yucky. I'm not even touching it."

The meal continued on, with Miranda carrying most of the conversation. Nick seemed content to listen to her chatter. By dessert, she had yawned several times and declined the sherbet placed in front of her. Tamara picked her up and carried her to get her bath.

"Nicky?" Miranda called over Tamara's shoulder. She paused in her exodus.

"Yes?"

"Will you tuck me in bed?"

Pain squeezed Tamara's heart. She waited for Nick's answer.

"If you want me to, I will," he said. Tamara didn't look back at him.

It's just for tonight. He's not going to be part of her life. He just wanted to meet her. He's doing that.

Within half an hour, Miranda was in bed, her wig back in place. Her clothes and cape had been replaced with her Super Cooper nightgown. Sandy had kissed her goodnight and withdrawn to her downstairs room. Tamara hovered at the doorway and watched Nick, still in suit and tie sitting on the chair next to her daughter's bed. He stood and walked over to her wall where a wooden ukulele hung.

"What's this?"

"Uka-lay-luh. What do you think?" Miranda gave Nick a no nonsense look.

He carefully lifted it from the holder and positioned the instrument against his chest.

"Do you know how to play it? Cause if you don't, you're not allowed to touch it, or you'll tear it up."

"I won't tear it up." He fingered the frets and strummed. "I know one song. Want to hear it?"

"Yes."

"Promise not to laugh if I mess up? It's been a long time since I sang."

"I'll try."

He played a few notes. It sounded like the Goodnight song, a lullaby Tamara had sung to her daughter many times.

Tamara's throat tightened. She crossed her arms, leaned on the threshold, and watched her daughter who studied this man whom she'd been told was her grandfather.

"Good night, sweet one, another day has come and gone. And now…."

"And now," Miranda echoed the chorus.

"The moon will shine a soft light on us throughout the night."

"The night," she added in her little girl melodic voice.

They sang together, and at the end of the song, Miranda yawned. "That was pretty good."

"Thanks."

She turned on her side toward the wall. "Will you be here when I wake up in the morning?"

"I guess I could be if you like."

"Mom will make us pancakes. Goodnight, Nicky."

He sat for a moment watching her, and then he sighed and stood. Carefully he laid the ukulele on the dresser top and walked out of the room, brushing by Tamara without even looking at her. She followed him into the living room where he strode over to the window and looked out. He raised his hand to his face, and Tamara realized with amazement he was brushing away a tear.

Was it possible?

After a moment, he cleared his throat. "How does she know that song?"

"I sing it to her sometimes at night."

"How could you…." He shook his head and swiped his eye again. "I…I used to sing it to Reg when he was just a little guy. Before his mother and I divorced." Nicolaus faced her. "It seems incredible that you would sing it to Miranda."

"It's not so incredible. You and I are the same age. The song was really popular when we were in school. There're only three chords. You know that was the big thing when we were…what? Fifteen?" Tamara approached him. She almost reached up to touch his arm, offer comfort, but she resisted. The last time they had touched….

"Yeah."

"And remember we watched that movie at the hotel. It was one we both had seen from when we were young."

His green eyes roved over her face. "Reg used to suck his thumb. 'Sing me the song, Daddy' he'd say. I never knew—couldn't imagine back then—how bad things would get, how much of a stranger he became to me, and no matter what I did or said, he saw it as an attack on him." Tears filled his eyes and spilled onto his cheeks. "He died hating me."

Tamara pulled a tissue out of her pocket. She lifted her hand, then lowered it. Finally giving in to the urge, she dabbed at his cheeks. "I'm sorry. I'm sorry that it still hurts even now."

"For two years Reg dropped out of sight. I'd call Brenda to see if she'd heard from him, but she always said no. Then when I got the news that they both had been killed, I found out he'd been living with her for over a year. Brenda didn't even have the decency to tell me."

"That was very unkind of her."

He heaved a breath, trying to collect himself, Tamara thought.

"I've never.... I don't know what's wrong with me. I don't cry. This is ridiculous. You must think...."

"I think that your son died, and your heart is broken. I think finding out he has a daughter and spending time with her must be very difficult."

A guttural cry erupted from him, and Tamara enfolded him in her arms. He tucked his face in her shoulder and wept as if he'd just received the news of his son's death. Tamara patted him and whispered words of comfort. And after a while he quieted, but he didn't let her go.

"I'm sorry."

"Don't be."

"I shouldn't have been so cruel to you when we met. I was a son of a bitch."

"I understand, and it's okay."

"It's not. I should have gone right then to the hospital to

give her the marrow."

Tamara tightened her arms around him. "You came around. That's the important thing."

He shifted and would have stepped away, but Tamara wouldn't release him. She drew her head back and gazed up at him. "That's the important thing. Okay?"

He nodded once, and his attention went from her eyes to her lips. Or, did Tamara imagine it? No. No. She'd seen a similar look in the hotel room, felt that response inside of her body from the nearly palpable vibrations emanating from him. Hormones. Intense emotions. It all contributed to the illusion of intimacy. They'd connected, and—

He swooped down and captured her lips, the contact firm and sure. He broke contact and gaged her reaction. Tamara was too shocked to give him any sign, but her body was shouting, *more!* He must have heard it because he lowered his head and kissed her again, slower this time, tentative as if he were sampling wine. Just a taste to decide. A hesitation, then Tamara deepened the kiss and took what he was offering before he came to his senses and went running out the door.

He drew away from her in a swift motion. "Why did you sleep with me? Why are you kissing me now? Is it so I'll give Miranda my blood?"

Tamara dropped her gaze. She didn't want him to see everything she planned and didn't plan. She chose her words carefully. "My intention in flying down to Atlanta was to talk you into donating, but you acted interested, which was surprising and flattering. I've never.... What I mean is, it's been a long time since anyone wanted to be with me. And even if anyone was interested, I don't have time to pursue it, or even the interest. Miranda is my life." She finally looked up and into those disturbingly beautiful and searching eyes. "I would do anything to save her. I'm sorry if having intercourse with me confused the issue, but that time together in the hotel room allowed you to ask me medical questions without the emotional baggage of suspicion of my motives. Yes, I could have told you who I was, but you wouldn't have felt free to talk to me and let me talk to you parent to parent. If my daughter lives, I have no regrets."

Nick sucked in air through his teeth. "I will take the test tomorrow. If can give her the marrow, I will do it no matter what happened or happens between you and me."

"Okay."

"So, if I ask to stay the night—with you— your answer will not be about getting a donor for Miranda."

"Her life means everything to me."

"I told you I'd give her the marrow."

"You will if you can, but if you're not a match, then it's a moot point."

"Then we'll find a match."

"I hope so. I hope to God there is one."

Nick placed his hands on her shoulders. "We will find one."

Tamara didn't like his use of *we*. She didn't want him to take this on as a project or a responsibility. "You can stay the night with me, but we can't get involved."

Nick's mouth lifted at the corner but whether it was a sneer or a smile, Tamara couldn't tell.

"What about tomorrow night? Can I stay then, as long as we aren't involved?"

Desire unfurled in her belly. Was he saying he wanted them to start sleeping together? For how long? She adopted a nonchalant tone, one she sometimes used at the hospital when things became intense. "You live in Charleston and work downtown. Staying nights here isn't practical, and anyway, I don't want Miranda thinking you're going to be a fixture in her life. Because you're not."

"What if I want to be?"

Tamara stepped out of his reach. Emotions swirled in her mind—how handsome he was. How dangerous. How the gentle scene in Miranda's bedroom twisted her heart because Nick could so quickly endear Miranda to him. Tamara had witnessed how ruthless he could be. He'd treated Tamara like a nobody at first. He'd met her and in the same evening he'd had sex with her. He had no heart, no matter how charming he acted toward her daughter. With the unresolved grief he had toward his son, Nick represented a mess Tamara did not have the energy or time to sort out.

Even now, the memory of the night in Atlanta elicited longing. But emotionally, it was too much. The only reason to sleep with him was to get pregnant. If he knew, he wouldn't agree. He said he'd be a donor, but he wasn't thinking sperm.

"You want control? Fine. You can have me on demand as long as it doesn't interfere with Miranda."

Nick folded his arms over his chest. "You'd prostitute yourself that way?"

"I'll be whatever you want me to be. But I don't want her getting close to you and then you deciding you don't like being a grandfather. Her physical and mental wellbeing is my top priority. My only priority."

A muscle worked in his jaw. He'd thought he'd provoke her by calling her a prostitute. But Tamara recognized his tactic. He was a lawyer. Of course, he played dirty.

"What time does Miranda wake up?"

"A little after six usually."

"I'll be here at a few minutes before six," He paused for a few seconds then his voice dropped, "Tomorrow."

He spoke the word as he had the night in Atlanta when he'd thought it was her name. Goose bumps rose on her skin.

Nick turned around and walked out of the room toward the entrance foyer. Tamara watched him leave. She heard the front door open, then close. She exhaled, not realizing she'd been holding her breath.

Chapter Seven

Can I bring anything? Nick had texted her at a quarter to five the next morning.

Tamara had ignored the text.

She didn't need anything from him, but the news that he was a match for her daughter.

Miranda woke up at five-thirty. She had come into the kitchen, her mostly bald head caused Tamara's chest to tighten. The little girl had refused to let them cut her remaining hair or shave her head. Because she wore her Super Cooper wig most of the time, seeing her without it was still a shock.

"Where's Nicky?" The words came out around the thumb plugging her mouth.

"He'll be here in a little while." Tamara opened the oven door and put in a breakfast casserole.

"He said he'd be here when I woke up." The ridge of her brow lowered—where her eyebrows used to be.

"I told him you don't wake up until six. He said he'd be here by then. Why don't you lie back down for a few minutes?"

Miranda declined, of course, with her best four-year-old "No."

"All right. Then go get dressed. He will be here soon."

When the doorbell rang, Tamara answered the summons. This morning, Nick wore a blue striped shirt with a blue silk tie and dark pants. His formal attire led Tamara to conclude he would go straight to work after the breakfast date. He held a basket with several bottles of fruit juice protruding from the top.

"You didn't respond to my text, and I didn't want to

come empty handed."

Tamara stood back and opened the door wider. "Come in. We'll eat in the kitchen."

"Hi." Miranda appeared. She'd dressed in one of her princess dresses though Super Cooper's hair and cape were in place.

"Good morning."

"Where'd you go?"

Nick stepped into the foyer, and Tamara closed the door behind him. She took Miranda's hand in hers and led the way into the kitchen.

From the heavy footfalls behind her, Nick followed. "I went home."

Miranda looked over her shoulder at him. "You coulda stayed here, you know."

"Thanks. I don't think there's room."

"Sure, there is. You can sleep in Mama's bed."

Tamara kept walking, cringing inwardly at her daughter's suggestion.

"She stays with me in my room so she's not even using her bed right now. Right, Mama?"

"Mr. Pack can't stay here, sweetie. It's not appropriate." They entered the kitchen. Tamara went to the cabinet and opened it. She reached for a coffee cup and poured coffee in it.

"His name's Nicky. He is my grand father." She enunciated the two words as if she were still trying them out. "You're my grand father, right, Nicky?"

"Yes."

"Meemee stays here, and she is my grandmother. Grand mother."

Tamara carried the cup to the table and placed it next to the plate where Nick would be sitting. "Sit down, Miranda."

"I want Nicky sitting next to me."

Tamara slid the cup to the place where she usually sat.

"Where does Mommy sit?" Nick settled on the chair as he posed the question to her daughter.

"There."

Tamara sat down across from Miranda and picked up her own coffee cup sipping from it.

"Then Mommy should sit here."

"She doesn't mind, do you, Mommy?"

"No. It's just a chair." It wasn't really true. Tamara minded a lot. She didn't want Nick sitting in her chair. She didn't even want him in the house, but all of this was until they found out if he could donate the marrow.

Then he'd be out of their lives for good.

****

After breakfast, Miranda looked up at Nick. "Can you play with me in my treehouse?" Her treehouse was actually a loft over the sitting room. Tamara had converted it to a play area painting the walls with branches and decorating the beam at the balcony to look like a tree trunk.

"Mr. Pack has to leave." Tamara picked up their plates and carried them over to the sink. "He has a long drive to get to work."

"His name is Nicky, Mom. He's my grand father."

Irritation buzzed around Tamara's head like a pesky mosquito. Tamara turned on the faucet and began to wash the dishes. "Nicky cannot stay. I have to go to work in a few minutes myself."

"But Meemee is here, and Nicky could stay with me until she gets up, couldn't you, Nicky?"

"I'd like to stay, but…."

"Oh, good. Come here, and let me show you my treehouse." The little girl stood up and pulled him to his feet. Obediently, he allowed her to lead him out of the room.

Where was the man who had called her delusional outside of his office and told her to take another elevator? Where was the man who'd callously bedded her then walked away? How come Nicolaus Pack forgot to bring his spine with him to breakfast this morning?

She had to get him out of the house. He was not going to be Miranda's grandfather. Tamara had told him that.

Tamara moved the griddle to the sink and cleaned it. She wiped her hands on a tea towel then went to throw Nicky out when Sandy walked in the room.

"Good morning." The speculative gleam in her eye greeted Tamara.

Tamara ignored it.

"Nick's here."

"He's leaving now."

"Did he stay the night?"

"Of course not."

"He and Miranda are up in her treehouse. Why don't you let him stay a little longer?"

"Because he's not her friend or her playmate. He's a forty-four year old man whom I don't know very well. He needs to leave."

"He's her grandfather. This is good for her."

"No. She doesn't need a grandfather, especially not one like him."

"He seems like a really nice man, Tamara."

"He's got issues. I—we—don't need that in our lives right now."

"Everyone has issues, honey."

"Mom, please. Trust me to know what is good for my daughter." Tamara limped out of the room hoping it would end the discussion. Ascending the staircase, she heard Nick's voice reading one of Miranda's storybooks. When Tamara reached the landing, she saw Nick sitting on the window seat with Miranda sitting across from him, her back leaned up against the cushion and her thumb in her mouth. The sun hadn't risen yet, but the sky promised an immanent dawn, and the soft light provided an appealing backdrop to the serene scene. They weren't touching, but the connection was nearly palpable. Miranda's gaze wasn't on the book, but on the man's face who was reading it. A lump of anger arose in Tamara's throat. He had no right to be here. None.

"The bunny jumped," he read. "She jumped on the log and looked. Was her cotton tail there? No, it was not."

"Let me see."

Nick turned the book toward her. "Do you see her cotton tail?"

She grinned around her thumb and shook her head.

"Wonder where that cotton tail is?"

"Turn the page."

Dutifully, he did. "The bunny jumped. She jumped to the pond where the tall cattails grew. Maybe her cotton tail was hiding with the cattail plants, but, no. Nothing but a dragon fly resting on the stalk."

"Nick," Tamara said. "It's time to go."

Nick didn't even acknowledge Tamara had said anything. He smiled at his granddaughter and held the book to her. "You sure you don't see that cotton tail?"

Miranda's eyes cut to Tamara then to the book.

"Here. Hold it. Look really, really well." He placed the book in her hands and rose.

"No, Nicky. Don't leave."

"I'll be right back."

Oh, no, you won't.

Nick's hard gaze pierced Tamara's as he walked toward her. Without pausing, he moved past her and descended the staircase. At the bottom he turned and leaned back against the end of the banister, his profile hard. Why was he standing there? She'd asked him to leave.

Tamara's foot still twinged at times when she walked though she'd quit wearing the boot after the first week, opting instead to wear a cloth brace under her sock. The slight pain hindered her gait when she moved quickly, making her feel more clumsy. She placed her foot on the last stair going past him toward the front door, but he didn't follow.

"Nick, you will leave now."

He tucked his chin down, watching her. But otherwise, he didn't move.

Tamara folded her arms over her chest and retraced her steps. She didn't like this battle of wills. "You've met her. You had dinner, and now breakfast."

He still didn't speak until the tension was so thick, Tamara had to fight not to fidget. What was it going to take to get him to leave already?

"I want to finish reading the story to her. It's not that long. You're being unreasonable." He spoke softly, so that Tamara had to move closer to understand him.

She took one step closer. "Why are you doing this? Is it to prove you can?"

"It's just a story, Tamara."

"No, it isn't, and you know it. Don't do this."

"It's just a story," he repeated.

Didn't he realize how every minute he spent with Miranda was building a connection? "Maybe it's just a story to you, but it isn't to her. She doesn't need to get attached to you."

"She's an amazing little girl."

What did he mean? Tamara nodded. "Thank you for coming back for breakfast. If you want me to set up an appointment for you to get the blood test, text me later, and I will make the arrangements." She hoped this was enough of an invitation to get him to leave.

"You say she's vulnerable, and upsetting her isn't good for her. I think leaving before I finish reading her the book could be construed as uncaring. I believe this would upset her, and I don't want to do that. Therefore, I am going back upstairs and finish the story. Afterward, I will leave."

All kinds of panic bells rang in Tamara's head. Nick turned and placed his foot on the first stair, but Tamara placed her hand on his arm. It took everything in her to speak. "Please, Nick."

He paused, and his face turned to hers. He was so close. The proximity made her a little dizzy.

"Please, what?" he murmured. The tone reminded of her of the fevered whispers he had breathed against her skin a couple of weeks before.

Tamara shook off the memory. "Please don't go up there. Just leave."

"You know some things about me…" the glitter in his eyes left her little doubt about the things he meant. How he looked in the dim light of the hotel television as he stood next to the bed. The rasp of his whiskered cheek against hers. The taste of his skin. "But here's something you probably don't know. I like to finish what I start, and I also keep my word. I told her I would be right back, and you're not going to make a liar out of me." His gaze dropped to her hand still resting on his arm. "At least, not today."

He ascended the stairs effectively breaking Tamara's contact with him. She turned to go into the kitchen and saw Sandy stood in the room. How long had she been there?

"Mom, I've got to go."

"All right."

"Nick is to leave as soon as he finishes reading that book to Miranda. Can I count on you to make sure that happens?"

"I wish—"

"Can I count on you to make sure that happens?"

Sandy sighed. "All right."

"And do not let him promise Miranda he will come back later." Tamara picked up her backpack and shouldered it.

Sandy shook her head indicating she thought Tamara's request unreasonable. "How am I supposed to go up there and be the promise police?"

"If she asks him to come back, interject and say he can't, then distract her."

Still uneasy, Tamara left the house and arrived at the hospital with only five minutes to spare. She withdrew her cell phone from her bag and laid it on the desk top and opened her designated drawer and placed the rest of her belongings inside. Glancing at the electronic board on the wall, she saw only four patients of the capacity 18 rooms with spaces in the hallway for 7 more if needed.

Shelly, the overnight doctor, swiveled in his chair to face her.

"Good job house cleaning before I got here," Tamara said.

"What can I say? I'm that good."

She smiled at him, but didn't comment. Working in the emergency department provided a lot of opportunity for expecting the unexpected and realizing how little control any of the staff carried over who would come in for help. Sometimes the shift was a circus. Other times it ran smooth with no problems whatsoever.

"What are you leaving for me?"

"The trauma in 2 is going up to ortho until surgery, so nothing there for you to do. There's a psych patient in 4, and her case worker has been called, but he's coming from Lincoln County, so maybe by noon she can be discharged. 17 is an overflow, and 8 arrived about twenty minutes ago from triage. Cole is in there now. You ought to buy me breakfast for how easy you're starting."

The bell rang indicating the EMTs were at the ambulance entrance with a patient, and a new name had appeared on the board for room 6. It might be starting easy, but it probably wouldn't stay that way.

Tamara logged on the computer in front of her and brought up the patient census. The patient's presenting problem was chest pain, and he was 51.

Cole, the nurse, approached Tamara's desk with the pink ECG paper in his hand. He held it out to her. "Good morning," he said.

"Thank you." She took the test results and studied the tracings.

"How's your foot?" he asked.

"Fine."

"Is that the doctor fine, the woman fine, or an actual fine?"

Tamara stood up and motioned for Cole to move. "Don't start with me this morning."

He moved out of her way, but followed her as she walked to room 8. "Did you have a follow up?"

"Don't need one. It's healing well." Tamara gave a perfunctory knock on the sliding glass door and walked into the patient room. A man reclined on the bed with shirt off, the lead pads still attached to spots on his chest and torso. "Hello, I'm Doctor Wallace."

A woman who sat on a chair next to the bed stood. The wife, Tamara decided.

"What brings you here?"

"Nothing," the patient said.

"His chest has been hurting for three days. When he couldn't catch his breath this morning, I drove him here."

The man shot an irritated glance at the woman.

Tamara addressed him. "Has your chest been hurting?"

His sigh came through loud and but a little muddled as she listened to his chest with the stethoscope. "Yes."

Hmmm. Tamara moved the diaphragm of the instrument to listen to his back.

"Have you been coughing?"

"Some."

Tamara's cell phone vibrated in her pocket, but she ignored it as she continued the examination.

When she left the room, she pulled her cell out and looked at the screen. A text from Nick.

It read: *Are you available?*

Of course, she wasn't available. She was working. Tamara placed the phone back in her pocket and went to chart her visit. By the time she'd opened the patient's chart, another text came through on her phone. Irritation buzzed Tamara's mind. So arrogant.

She typed up her notes and pulled out her phone.

It's about the blood test.

Tamara huffed and texted back. *What about it?*

Can I get it here?

Tamara squinted at the screen. What an idiotic message. She didn't know where he was.

Where's here?

County Hospital. ER lobby.

No, he wasn't.

Why did you come here?

Thought you could get me in and out quicker.

Tamara snorted. What a short memory he had.

He had made her wait two hours before having his secretary tell Tamara he couldn't keep the appointment.

Also, seems more efficient to get the test closer to Miranda. Figured she gets her treatments here since the children's hospital is here too.

Tamara's anger melted away. He'd thought out where Miranda got her treatment. He was right, of course. Miranda did get her chemo here, and having the blood test here made it a lot easier to get the results. Tamara laid her phone aside and looked up the extension of the lab on the other side of the hospital. She called and asked for reception to get blood work drawn on him ASAP and flag it for Miranda's file.

"Dr. Wallace?"

She looked up at Helen, one of the nurses.

"Four is ready for you."

Sorry, Nick. You'll have to wait a few more minutes. Tamara stood up and walked past the nurse's station.

Bonita, the unit clerk sat behind the divider with the phone at her ear. "Dr. Wallace, there's a phone call for you." Her eyebrows rose speculatively. "Nicolaus Pack. He's says he's family."

Family? Tamara tutted in annoyance. The man had no patience whatsoever. He didn't even give her time to get him worked in at the hospital lab, and he was *not* family.

"He's in the ER lobby. Call Angelo in guest services and ask him to escort Nick to the outpatient registration desk for some lab work."

"Don't you want to talk to him?"

"No. I don't."

****

Nick leaned against the wall of the lobby holding the cell phone to his ear while a message informed him of the benefits of being a patient here. Anger began to surface. He didn't have all day to spend waiting while Dr. Wallace decided if he was worthy enough for her time. Nick didn't understand her. She'd been so warm and inviting the night he'd met her, and now she treated him like shit.

Just like a woman. She manipulated him to get what she wants then pulls an attitude.

Considering what she'd done, Nick thought he'd acted graciously after he'd gotten over the shock of seeing her walk into his office. He's been the epitome of a gentleman. He'd been kind to Miranda and Tamara's mother. No one could fault him for anything he'd said or done since finding out about his granddaughter.

He wanted to help. He wanted to give her the marrow. God, he hoped he could. Even though he hated needles, hated being poked and prodded, couldn't stand hospitals. Even the smell of being here brought back memories of the night he'd been escorted out of Reginald's room when he'd coded and they'd had to do CPR.

The smell of blood and death had gagged him.

Stop. Stop it.

"Hi. Are you Nicolaus Pack?"

Nick looked at the young woman in a white uniform top and maroon scrub pants. "Yes."

She smiled and gestured for him to follow her. "I'm Bonita. I'll take you to the lab."

Nick fell into step next to her.

"Tamara isn't available?" They walked out of the lobby, down a hallway, and turned the corner down another hallway.

"No, but she wanted to make sure you had someone to escort you to the lab. You say you're family?"

"Yes."

"Close family?" Bonita studied his face as if she were attempting to look for clues.

So, Bonita was fishing for information. Nick smiled. "Very close."

"Her daughter...?"

"It's complicated. I'm sure you understand."

"Yes." She laughed briefly. "Miranda favors you. I knew when I saw you that you had to be related to her. We're all hoping she's going to make a complete recovery. She's a neat little girl."

"Yes, she is."

They approached a reception area with chairs and a window. Bonita stood in front of it. "Hi, Allen. This is Nicolaus Pack. Dr. Wallace sent him here for some lab work."

The man behind the glass nodded. He stood and opened the door leading to the lobby. "Come right in. Dr. Wallace wants you ASAP."

Nick chuckled.

Hardly.

****

Two days.

Two days late didn't mean anything necessarily. Tamara had been two days late before. Now, if she didn't start her period today, then, yes, that would be cause for concern.

Or, not concern exactly.

Elation and panic arm wrestled for dibs in her chest.

She couldn't really be pregnant, could she?

It was absurd. She was 44 years old. No way she could get pregnant after intercourse one time with Nick. He was as old as she was. His sperm count was likely low, and it was doubtful that Tamara was even ovulating each month. Statistically, it should take her months to get pregnant. Years even. If at all.

She usually had cramps before her menses. Tamara paused and focused on her abdomen. No pain. Not even a hint of discomfort.

It could be stress causing the amenorrhea. Anxiety about Miranda. About Nick. The cancer. Everything.

Just this morning the lab had called and said they hadn't been able to get conclusive results on his blood test. The sample had been corrupted. He'd have to give another sample.

She'd texted him and advised him to go to the hospital in Charleston for the test, but he'd texted back and asked if she'd meet him at the lab at Acorn County Hospital at four, the end of her shift.

She didn't need this today. Unless she started to bleed. Then he'd just be a necessary nuisance.

I might be pregnant.

"You okay?" Cole's question brought her out of her reverie.

Tamara looked up at him.

"Room 5 is ready for you. Little kid with NVD."

NVD. Nausea. Vomiting. Diarrhea. Tamara looked at the census on her computer screen. A four-year-old. The same age as Miranda.

"Tamara?"

"Can I see you in the breakroom for a minute?" She said already walking toward the door. She swiped her badge and opened the door when it gave her the green light indicating she'd gained entry. No one else was in there. Tamara opened the refrigerator and picked up a water bottle.

"Confidential, okay?"

Cole nodded once, his gaze steady on hers.

"I need a pregnancy test."

"For which patient?"

"For the one standing in here with you."

He didn't even hesitate. "All right."

"No one can know."

He moved is head from side to side as if working how he could get lab work done discreetly. "All right. I'll draw it. We'll put a number on the tube, and I'll take it myself to the lab."

"Thanks."

Cole nodded and left. Tamara breathed in and out a few times.

Calm. Calm. If I am, this is a good thing. I wanted to have another baby. I just haven't gotten around to it because of Miranda. It could be a very good thing if the baby is a match. I could use the cord blood. That could be enough for a cure.

If I am.

Chapter Eight

Tamara had wanted to find out the test results, but got busy with patients. By noon, she still hadn't had her lunch break. She walked by Cole on her way to see a patient. He looked at her.

And she knew that he knew.

I'm pregnant.

She set aside the knowledge and cared for her patient. Then she went to the physician's station and called up the lab results on her computer.

Her hCG level was....

Wow. Elevated.

Non-pregnant women would have 5 or below.

I am pregnant.

She looked at the other levels. Iron. Hemoglobin. Glucose. All looked good. She'd need to take another test in a few days to compare her hCG level to today's result.

Okay. Now, I know. I'll finish work and think about it later.

Later came when she concluded her shift, opened the lounge door, and met Cole's eyes. He leaned against the hallway wall with his arms crossed over his chest.

"Hi," he said, his compassionate expression nearly undoing her.

Tamara stumbled forward, and he steadied her, placing his hands on her shoulders.

"I'm thinking the dazed look in your eyes means you saw the results."

"Umm…yeah." She blew out a breath and straightened her glasses on her nose.

"This is a good thing, Tamara. Isn't it?"

"Yes. Yes, it is. It's still very early though. I don't want to…get too excited about it." Oh, my gosh.

"How early?"

"Eighteen days exactly."

"You'll take good care of yourself."

"I have to. I want this. I really want this." Since Miranda had been diagnosed there had been nothing but bad news, fear, and dread. Finally, she had something positive to grasp onto.

"Good." Cole stepped away from her, and they began to walk toward the exit.

"Dr. Wallace?" Bonita said and walked toward her with Nick behind her, dressed in a dark blue suit, a snowy white shirt, and a tie the most beautiful shade of green she'd ever seen.

Well, except for the green of his eyes. Those eyes met hers. All of the nerve endings in Tamara's body buzzed, as if she had gotten an electric shock.

"Nick said he was meeting you at four. I hope it's okay I brought him back."

Nick's attention moved to Cole who was walking back toward the patient rooms, then Nick's gaze settled on her.

Oh, Nick. What you've done to me, for me.

Emotion rose up so strong that Tamara found it hard to swallow or even breathe for a few seconds.

"Dr. Wallace?" Bonita said, a hint of concern entering her voice.

"Yes. Yes. It's fine." Tamara marched forward, putting aside all of the hopes and fears of this new revelation and focusing on the task before them. Blood test. "Hi, Nick. Shall we go to the lab?"

She felt and heard him move from behind her, his loafers making that same assured stride she'd heard those few weeks ago the first time she'd ever seen him.

Then he was beside her. She caught a sweet subtle scent of men's cologne. It felt good to be walking with him through the hospital, smelling him, feeling the close proximity of his body near hers.

"What was wrong with test?"

Tamara's heart jumped. "What?"

"What was wrong with the blood test?"

"Oh." She laughed softly, and Nick stopped.

Tamara pivoted and looked at him. He glared at her.

"You think it's funny that they have to take more blood? You're not doing this just to test me, are you? To see how far I'm willing to go, how much I'm willing to bleed for your daughter?"

"No, Nick. Of course not."

"What was wrong with the sample?"

"I don't know. Sometimes, the blood is corrupted. The tube might have broken or it wasn't sealed well. They try to be careful, but sometimes mistakes happen. And we have to be very sure."

A muscle twitched in his jaw. Tamara realized he was grinding his teeth.

"It will be all right."

"I don't like being lied to, and I expect you to be upfront with me."

Tamara's heart banged against her ribs. Had he somehow found out about the pregnancy test? Impossible. But anyway, Tamara did not think it appropriate for them to have this conversation in the hallway. A consult room lay ahead and Tamara looked inside. No one occupied it, so she walked inside and stood at the door.

"What are you doing? This isn't the lab," Nick said as he walked inside the room.

Tamara closed the door and resisted the urge to move away from him. Her body jangled as if her skin remembered, aha. This was the one who loved this skin so, who kissed and licked and worshiped....

"This is where I work. I would rather not have my personal...." Affairs wasn't the word she wanted, so she searched her mind for another one. "business discussed in the hallway. Now, what is it I have lied to you about? How am I not being upfront with you?"

"What's the policy here about sexual relationships? Are you allowed to be involved with your co-workers?"

"What's your point?"

"You slept with me."

"You don't work here."

His eyes glittered with anger, but on that night he'd gazed at her with a softness, a vulnerable quality about him when he'd talked about his son.

"Does your boyfriend know?"

"I don't have a boyfriend, not that it's any of your business."

"Do you let all the male staff fondle you, or just that guy in the ER?"

"What guy?"

Nick turned and prowled the room. Tamara wondered if he paced that way in the court.

"That guy in the scrubs who had his hands all over you in the ER."

Cole? Tamara laughed. "You're kidding, right? He's a nurse, and he did not have his hands all over me. I stumbled in the hallway, and he caught me."

"I saw the way he was looking at you."

"Just because we…we've…." Tamara felt her face heat. "Atlanta does not give you any right over me, Nick. Now I appreciate that you think Cole is interested, but look at me. I'm a fat, nerdy doctor, and he's at least ten years younger than me."

Nick touched his finger to his chin and scratched his jaw. He studied her for a moment until the air popped between them. Tamara looked away.

"Fat, nerdy doctor?" The silky tone drew Tamara's eyes for a couple of seconds before skittering away again.

Nick approached her, and Tamara turned to the door.

"We better go," she said.

"Nerdy? Maybe, but I find fault with the other description. Fat isn't an accurate term. I've seen you. I know." Nick was close now. Tamara swore she felt the heat from his body. She closed her eyes. If she leaned back, he'd be there touching her, her back against his chest. Close. So close. "Curvy. Voluptuous." His voice dropped, and his breath stirred her hair. "Rubenesque."

Suspicion nudged her. First he was angry, then he was seductive. What was he doing? What was this really about?

She cleared her throat and used her most authoritative doctor voice. "Step back, please."

She felt the coolness of the room when he did so. Tamara turned away from the door and faced Nick. Setting aside the desire he stirred in her, the irritation of him wanting to lay claim on her, and the uneasiness of knowing she was pregnant, and he was the biological father.

He returned her look, but there was an edginess to him. A nervousness.

Why?

Aha. She recognized it.

"You don't like hospitals, do you?"

He stilled. "No. And I don't relish the thought of being jabbed with a needle twice in one week."

"Are you afraid of needles?"

He made a sound of disgust. "Afraid of needles."

"The staff here are very professional. There's nothing to be worried about."

"I've already done this once this week. The bruises on my arm where they butchered me last time is proof. Not to mention your professional staff compromised the blood sample, so I don't believe you."

"Let me see."

The corner of his mouth quirked and he unbuttoned his jacket and removed it. His eyes bore into hers, and Tamara dropped her gaze, remembered when he had disrobed in front of her before.

Oh, that beautiful night.

I'm pregnant. I'm wonderfully pregnant.

Tamara put the thought out of her mind. She could gush

later when she was alone.

He rolled up his sleeve, and Tamara saw the bruises he mentioned. She stepped forward and held his forearm running her finger down his skin tracing the darkened areas there.

"No wonder you're scared."

"I'm not scared. I just don't like being someone's pin cushion because they can't get a vein."

Tamara moved closer to him, pushing on one vein then another one gaging which would be a good one to harvest the blood. The larger vein moved aside as she pressed down. She set down her backpack which she'd hooked over one arm, then placed her fingers around his bicep and watched to see any change in the veins.

Oh, my goodness, he had nice biceps. He had to work out. No one developed muscles like these just lifting law books. Tamara certainly didn't verbalize her thoughts. In the quiet of the moment, she heard his intake and expulsion of breath. She knew if she looked into his face, she'd be lost. If he closed the space between them and kissed her, she'd allow it. Even now, tentacles of longing reached out to him, wanting to bring him in, to her. This man who had made love to her so sweetly, had given her a baby, who had sung to her daughter, and was willing to take a second blood test though the first experience had obviously been painful.

"I'll be sure you get a good phlebotomist. A really good one." Tamara picked up her backpack and unzipped it. Retrieving her phone, she called Marion, the nursing supervisor for the hospital. "Hi, Marion, this is Dr Wallace."

"Hi, what's up?"

"I have a patient with me who took a blood test earlier this week. The test was inconclusive, so he needs to undergo another test, but he's a little reticent. It appears he has rolling veins and they had problems sticking him. I'd like him to have the best phlebotomist available right now. We're on our way to the lab."

"Kim Foster is excellent. I'll call her and send her there."

"Thank you." Tamara hung up the telephone and put it back in her backpack. "Let's go." She opened the door and began walking.

"I'm not afraid of needles."

She smiled. "What do you care what I think?"

He caught up to her and matched her stride. "Because you're the mother of my grandchild. I do care what you think."

Tears stung her eyes, surprising Tamara with their swift and unexpected presence.

He had no idea.

****

Becky Prescott, Tamara's OB/GYN agreed to see her as soon as she could get to the office. With the exam complete, Becky sat on the stool in the room while Tamara dressed in the curtained off alcove.

"Everything looks great. Your blood pressure is actually is little low, which is surprising." Becky typed as she spoke. Tamara surmised she was charting notes on the exam.

"I've always had low blood pressure."

"Yes, but at 44, your blood pressure ought to be rising, like the rest of us." She shrugged. "We'll watch it along with everything else, and do an amniocentesis later on to be sure there are no genetic issues with the baby."

"I want to know if the baby could be a match for Miranda. If so, we can bank the cord blood and use it for a transfusion."

The typing stopped. "Is this a donor baby?"

"I hope so."

"You didn't go to the fertility clinic again." The statement was almost a question. Becky's confusion stemmed from the fact that she had been the attending when Tamara had been implanted with the donor sperm five years ago.

"No, I did not. But I know there's a chance the baby could be a match, so if that's the case, I want to know as soon as possible."

"And if not, then what?"

"Then I have a baby, and we keep Miranda on the recipient list." Dressed, Tamara pulled back the curtain and sat on the only other chair in the room. "I've been wanting another baby, but I just haven't gotten around to it until now."

"And you found an alternative to the fertility clinic."

"I didn't use a turkey baster or another ob/gyn, if that's what you're asking. I... went the traditional route."

Becky laughed. "How traditional? I don't see a ring on your finger."

Tamara smiled in response. "Okay. Not quite that traditional. It was a risk to try at my age. I know that, but the opportunity presented itself, and I took a chance."

"You're absolutely sure of the date you conceived?"

"Yes."

"Well, we will keep a close watch on you, and hopefully in about 37 weeks, you'll deliver a healthy baby."

That evening, Tamara tucked Miranda in bed and moving up her Super Cooper hair, she kissed her daughter's forehead.

"Want me to sing you a song?"

"I want Nicky to sing to me. Can he come over?"

"No, honey. It's very late, and he lives almost an hour away. With traffic, it would be longer. By the time he could drive here, you'd be long asleep."

Irritation pricked at Tamara's throat. When she'd gone into the tree house tonight, she'd seen the name 'Nick' written on Miranda's dry erase board in the tree house. The letters looked childlike, but Miranda didn't know her letters well enough to write the name by herself. When Tamara had confronted Sandy about it, she'd shrugged.

"She asked how to spell his name, honey. So, I helped her write it."

"Mom, don't encourage her to keep thinking about him."

"She asked me, and anyway, I think it's good that she's interested in her ABCs, don't you?"

"Don't engage her about Nick. He can't be a part of our lives. Especially now."

"Why not especially now?"

Tamara didn't answer. She wasn't ready to disclose her secret yet. There'd be too much explaining as to how she got pregnant. It was tempting to say she'd kept her appointments at the fertility clinic, that she'd gone through with her plan to pursue pregnancy even though Miranda was sick. Of course, her mother probably wouldn't believe Tamara had gone down to Atlanta and gotten herself knocked up in one night either.

Tamara smiled. No one would believe she'd been so reckless.

"Mama!" Her daughter's voice brought her back to the present.

"What, honey?"

"When can he come back?"

"I don't know." In an attempt to distract Miranda from the subject, Tamara walked over to the bookcase. "Want me to read you a story?"

"I want Nicky to read me a story."

"How about this one?" She held up a favorite.

Miranda turned on her side, a sure sign she was getting sleepy. "All right," she said in a small voice.

By the time Tamara finished the book, Miranda was asleep. Tamara lifted the wig off her head and placed it in a basket they kept there for that purpose. The little girl's bare scalp struck Tamara as so foreign, as if someone had photoshopped the image she gazed upon. She rubbed her hand over Miranda's blanket covered leg.

She was going to be a big sister.

How would she react to a new baby? She'd been the center of Tamara and Sandy's world since she was born.

The next morning at the kitchen table, Tamara set a plate in front of her daughter. Two pieces of bacon, a pancake, and two orange wedges.

"Can Nicky eat breakfast with us?"

Miranda didn't answer. She was getting a little tired of hearing about Nicky and all of the places and events Miranda wanted him to be a part of.

"Mama. Mama. Mommy."

"Yes?"

"I want to see Nicky."

"No."

"I want to see Nicky."

"No. He lives almost an hour away."

"Can you call him?"

"Eat your breakfast."

"Please, can you call him? He misses me, I bet. If you call him, he would come see me."

"I want you to eat at least one piece of bacon and one slice of orange."

"Can I eat it and watch TV?"

"I suppose."

****

Nick stood before the mirror in the bathroom in his dress pants and undershirt. He razed the shaver across his cheek and chin. From the bedroom, his cell phone chirped, signaling a call. He picked up a towel and strode over to his nightstand.

The screen identified the caller as Tamara. Good. Maybe she had news about the blood test.

Nick slid his finger over the screen and answered.

"Nicky?" Miranda asked. "Nicky, will you come over again?"

Nick went back into the bathroom and finished his task—two more swipes ought to do it.

"Miranda? Where's your mommy, sweetheart?"

"She's in the kitchen," Miranda whispered. "Would you? Mommy says you're too far away, but I know you'd come see me if you missed me."

"Does Mommy know you're talking to me?" He rinsed the raiser and knocked the water out of it against the sink.

"Ummm... yes."

Nick smiled. The little stinker. She was lying.

He wiped his face with the towel and walked back in his bedroom to his closet. Choosing a shirt, he slid his arms into it and buttoned it. "Tell you what. I'll call your mom and see if we can work something out. All right?"

"Tell her she has to let you come see me. I miss you."

Nick's heart turned to goo in his chest. "I miss you, too. But you shouldn't use Mommy's phone unless she says it's okay."

"And you'll come see me."

"Miranda." Nick shook his head in amazement. "I can't promise anything, but I'll talk to your mom."

"I love you, Nicky."

A lump the size of the fifth street bridge lodged in Nick's throat. He swallowed once. Twice.

"I said I love you, Nicky. You're posed to say I love you too."

"I love you, too."

And he realized he really did.

They said their goodbyes, and Nick hung up the telephone. He walked over to his dresser and found a pair of socks. Sitting on the bed, he slipped them on his feet. A knock sounded on his open bedroom door.

"Yes?"

Devon, his sixteen-year-old son, stepped in the room. "Dad?"

"Yeah?"

"Umm, can I have some money for lunch? The school says my account's overdrawn."

Devon. His only surviving son. After Brenda and Reg died, Devon had come to live with him. Nick barely knew him because he'd been so young when they had divorced. But he was a good kid.

"Sure." Nick picked up his wallet from the dresser and pulled out a couple of twenties.

Devon stood in front of him, as if waiting for him to say something else, his brown eyed gaze struck Nick as soulful, sad.

"Do you need more than that? I'll put some money in your account this week, all right?

"I could use some gas money."

"Where's your check card?"

Devon shrugged. "That account's empty too. You told me to put the new tires on it."

"Oh, that's right. Sorry. I'll put more in there today." Nick pulled out his last two twenties and handed them over.

Devon turned and left the room.

Chapter Nine

"I'm sorry, Tamara." Dr. Thomas gazed at her regretfully. "I know you were hoping he would be a match."

She shrugged. "Yeah, well."

The oncologist's kind expression should have elicited comfort in Tamara, but it didn't. She didn't like being on the receiving end of a doctor's compassion. It was a role she wasn't used to. And she certainly didn't like it had taken them over a week to inform her Nick wasn't a match. There was such a thing as professional courtesy, and in this situation more than any other, he should abide by it.

"She has a good chance of going into remission even without a transplant."

"Her chances increase to nearly 100 percent with it."

He smiled. "That's true, but since there isn't a donor, we'll go forward with the treatment plan we've already discussed."

"Her numbers aren't good enough to have the chemo. How are we going to go forward with the treatment plan when she's too weak to do it?"

"We'll give her some blood. It will help."

"Give her the blood now, so we can get her numbers where they need to be and do the chemo."

"We could do that, yes, but it's really late in the day, and I'd want her to stay a few hours after for observation, and that's going to mean a hospital stay. Do you really want her to have to stay in the hospital tonight?"

"I can observe her. I sleep in her room every night."

Desperation threatened to squeeze the air out of her lungs. Tamara didn't want to wait for the next infusion. She wanted Miranda to get the chemo as soon as possible. They had to fight it with everything they had.

"I know this is difficult," he said.

What a dumb statement. Of course, it was difficult. Fred Thomas had children. Would he still spout the platitudes if it were his daughter's life in jeopardy? Tamara doubted it.

"Her white count should be lower. Her platelets should be higher. A lot higher. She shouldn't need blood now."

The doctor didn't reply—just stared at her. Tamara returned his look and waited for him to look away first. He didn't, but he did finally speak.

"Treatment is sometimes two steps forward, and one step back. Be patient."

"You and I both know the numbers are already indicating that the chemo isn't working."

"You let me worry about that."

Tamara stood up and glared at him. "I will let you do nothing of the sort. She may be your patient, but she is my daughter."

"Every patient is the son or the daughter of someone."

"Don't. Don't pull that on me."

"It's just a minor setback. I am treating Miranda as I would my own child, Tamara."

White hot anger tasted like bile in her throat. Anger at the cancer, and anger at the doctor who so calmly sat there as if the world wasn't about to come to an end.

She stared at him for a moment. "You'd better."

Tamara walked out of Dr. Thomas' office where she'd requested a private consult. She opened the exam room door and looked at her mom who sat on a vinyl chair with Miranda on her lap sucking her thumb.

"Let's go," Tamara said as she reached down and picked up her daughter.

"What did he say?" Sandy asked as she gathered up her purse and followed her.

"Nick's not a match, and the numbers aren't where they should be. I'll talk to you about it later."

Tamara didn't want Miranda to hear she was going to

have to get blood in the morning. Even though she had a PICC line in place, she often refused any kind of medical procedure, so the less she knew the better.

That evening after she had gotten Miranda settled in bed, she called Nick. He'd texted her a few times during the week to find out about the blood test. She figured she owed him a phone call at least to let him know. He picked up after three rings.

"Hi, it's Tamara."

"Hi."

"You're not a match."

He didn't reply for a moment, then finally. "Dammit. I was really hoping I would be."

Tamara's chest ached at his admission. "So, thanks for taking the test. Goodbye." She held the phone away from her ear to hit the end icon.

"Wait a min—"

She heard his voice even as she pressed the red circle. She hadn't really meant to hang up on him, but he couldn't help.

Her phone rang as his name lit up the screen. Tamara debated not answering it, but it was just putting off the inevitable conversation. He couldn't be a part of their lives. If he found out about the baby, it would complicate things. She didn't need complications right now.

She slid her finger across the screen and pressed the phone to her ear. "I didn't mean to hang up on you. I just don't see a reason to talk about it anymore."

"What about another donor?"

"If one is found, but that's not your problem."

"She's my granddaughter. It is my problem."

"She isn't your granddaughter. Your son made a donation at a sperm bank. That didn't make him a father, and it doesn't make you a grandfather."

"You were willing to let her be my granddaughter when you thought I could help her."

"Only as far as acknowledging the biology. Even if you

had been compatible, I never planned on there being a relationship."

"You're not the only one who's involved here."

"No, but I am the only one who has a say in who is in my daughter's life. I would never have contacted you if it hadn't been to save her life. You can't do it, so you don't have any further obligation."

"This is no longer about obligation. She needs me."

"No, she doesn't."

"Why don't you want me to be part of her life?"

"Because I don't."

"That's not a reason."

"It's the only one I'm willing to share with you."

"Tamara." His sigh filled her ear. "You can pretend that the night in Atlanta never happened, that it was just about convincing me to help Miranda, but I think it got to you. I got to you. Like you did me. I want to be honest with you because I want you to be honest with me. I want to know you. I want to be in Miranda's life. I want to mean something to you because Miranda already means something to me."

Miranda meant something to him. Not Tamara. There's no way someone like him could want someone like her. He was just reacting to knowing a part of his dead son lived on in a little girl. Who wouldn't be drawn to that?

And how would he react if he found out Tamara was pregnant?

"I can't give her the bone marrow, but I can help shoulder the burden of a sick child. I've got an appointment in Covington Pike early tomorrow. Why don't you let me come by the hospital, and we can have brunch? Let me help you, Tamara."

"I can't. I…can't do this. Nick, I don't have the energy for it. Please, just let it go."

"You don't have to do this by yourself. Let me love her too."

"It means a lot that you care so much for her already, but I've got all I can handle right now. And Miranda needs to get better, not worry about when she can see you again. I've got to put her needs first. Please don't contact me again. This needs to be it." Once again, Tamara ended the call, hoping, this time, he wouldn't call back.

And he didn't.

****

It was trauma day.

Ordinarily, the traumas didn't start arriving until after lunch when the weather was nice and warm and people awoke and took a drive in their cars or too fast on their all-terrain vehicles.

But on this brisk March morning, the temperature hovered just below freezing, and it began to sleet.

Diane, one of the ER nurses, walked past the ambulance entrance looking out of the closed automatic doors. "Brace yourselves, folks. I predict we're going to get slammed."

"Shut up, Diane," Taryn, the registrar yelled from her spot in front of room six. With her mobile computer, she could go from room to room and input patient information into the hospital system. "If you jinx us, I'm blaming you."

"It won't be my fault. Blame Mother Nature. I'm glad I got to work before this started."

Tamara reached for the telephone on her desk and dialed Sandy's number. Their appointment wasn't for an hour yet, but Tamara wanted to warn her about the conditions. When Sandy didn't pick up the telephone, Tamara texted her with her cell. In a few minutes, Sandy texted back.

Having problems. Miranda doesn't want to go.

Tamara grimaced at the message. She called again, and when her mother picked up, she didn't waste time on greetings. "Why did you tell her where you all were going?"

"I'm not going to lie to her. She asked me where we were going."

Tamara could hear her daughter crying in the background.

"Let me talk to her."

"Mommy wants to talk to you, honey."

"Noooo!!! Noooo, Meemee. I don't want to go. Ahhhhh." Her words crumbled into wails.

Helplessness wrapped itself around Tamara's chest.

"I don't know what to do with her."

Trauma alert. Four minutes, the overhead speaker announced. Simultaneously, Tamara's beeper alarmed. She unclipped it from her waistband and looked at the small screen.

22 y.o.f. MVC. Priority 2. ETA 4 Min by ground.

22 Year old female. Motor Vehicle Crash. Priority 2 meant it was not life threatening, but it could be serious, and they had 4 minutes to prepare for the arrival which was coming by ambulance.

Another trauma alert sounded overhead.

The pager beeped again. This time, an eight month old baby. Also, a priority 2, and the estimated time of arrival was 9 minutes.

Probably the baby belonged to the 22 year old woman. Same wreck.

"Mom, you should probably go ahead and get here. The weather's bad, and the roads are slick. Take your time, and you will be fine."

"Tamara, maybe we should reschedule."

"She needs that blood. I can't come get her. We just had two traumas called. Do whatever it takes, but get her here, and for God's sake, be careful."

"All right. Whatever it takes. Gotcha."

Tamara swiped her hand across her forehead. Her mother's tone meant that she had found her second wind to make it happen. Good, but still a breath of doubt breathed down her neck.

"Call or text me when you get to the Cancer Center." The Cancer Center was an adjacent section of the hospital.

"Will do. Don't worry."

Tamara stood and saw a group congregated outside of Trauma rooms one and two. The radiologists stood in the hallway with the portable X-Ray machine, and the nursing supervisor stood at the counter of the nurse's station. Two residents from the medical school in Huntington fidgeted outside of the exam room door.

"Mom, I've got to go." She hung up the telephone and went to do her job.

In forty minutes, a text moved across Tamara's cell phone screen that Sandy and Miranda had arrived at the cancer center, and all was well.

Well, good. All was well. Miranda had settled down, and they were where they needed to be.

Tamara had wanted to check on her daughter during the day, but they were so busy in the ER that she didn't even have time to stop for lunch. A text from Sandy at one in the afternoon had informed Tamara that Miranda had received the blood transfusion, and they would be able to leave by mid-afternoon.

At a few minutes past four, Tamara walked out of the hospital, intent on going home to her daughter. When she arrived at the house, Nick's car was in the driveway.

Fury blinded her for a couple of seconds.

He had no right. None. She'd told him to stay away. Not to contact them anymore. Who did he think he was?

Tamara pulled her SUV into the garage and shut off the engine. She exited the vehicle and hurried into the house. When she opened the door, Sandy stood inside the kitchen, a placating look on her face and her hands raised in a calming stance.

"Now, don't be upset."

"I don't want him here, and you knew that," Tamara spoke in a low, angry tone.

"I know, but I didn't know what else to do. She started calling out for him, so I thought he might could calm her down. I was just going to let him talk to her on the phone. That was it."

Tamara raised her gaze to the ceiling in a frustrated gesture. "Mom, she's four years old. You're the adult. Are you honestly telling me of all of the resources at your disposal, you chose him?"

"You said do whatever it took."

"I didn't mean that."

"He was wonderful. She calmed right down when he got here."

"What do you mean? She was upset after you came home?"

"No. He's been with her—us—all day."

"Oh, Mom. How could you?"

"You said she had to have the blood today." Fatigue blanketed Sandy's face, but Tamara ignored it. No matter what kind of day her mother had had, Tamara could top it. In addition to the four traumas they'd had, a cardiac arrest had come in that had resulted in a death. Tamara had had to tell a woman that the man she'd been married to for forty-two years was dead.

As was Tamara's routine, she went upstairs and showered.

Coming back downstairs, she was much calmer. What had happened today had happened. Mom had needed help. She'd called Nick. He had come to the rescue. Miranda had received the blood transfusion.

That's what mattered.

The television played a Super Cooper Show, one Tamara had seen at least twenty times. Black socked feet with ankles crossed sat atop the foot rest of the reclined chair, and there was Nick kicked back with Miranda curled in his lap, a scene of contentment. His chin rested atop of her wigged head, and his knowing expression alerted Tamara that he knew she'd be angry finding him here.

"Hi, Mommy," Miranda said around her thumb. "Look who came to see me today."

"I see that."

"They gave me new blood, and they put it in my straw. It's Super Hero blood to make me strong. And it didn't even hurt or make me throw up. And Nicky stayed with me the whole time, didn't you Nicky?"

"Hmm-hmm," he acknowledged, but he was watching Tamara as she stood in front of them.

Tamara bent down and kissed her daughter's sweet face. She realized as she did it how close Nick was, caught a faint whiff of his cologne mingled with Miranda's little girl smell, felt invisible drawstrings pulling her into him, but she ignored it.

"I love you. Will you come sit with me for a while? I've missed you."

Miranda held up her arms, and Tamara began to pick her up. Nick's gaze met hers, their green fire depth making her heart pump hard in her chest.

This is the father of the baby I'm carrying.

Tamara's hands connected to his body as she groped to get a good hold of her daughter. Straightening, she backed away and moved to the couch.

"Thank you, Nick. You can leave now." She sat down and looked into her daughter's face. Her color looked better already. Tamara pulled aside Miranda's shirt at the neckline and checked the PICC line near her collarbone. Miranda called it her "straw" because the staff used it to infuse medicine, or in today's case, blood.

The site looked good.

Nick had put his shoes on and stood. Miranda turned her head and looked up at him. "Can I have a hug before you go?" she asked.

Hadn't she had enough contact with him today?

Nick walked to the couch. He knelt down and gazed into Miranda's face. "I'm proud of you because you were a very brave girl today. But remember what we talked about. When you scream and cry and kick Meemee, it hurts Meemee, and it makes you feel bad, too. Promise me you're going to try not to do that the next time."

"Will you be here the next time?"

"I don't know. It just worked out that I was close by today, and I could come stay with you, but I won't always be able to do that. It doesn't mean I don't love you. It just means I can't come right then. But I want to hear a good report from Mommy and Meemee, all right?"

"All right."

He reached forward and hugged her, his dark blond hair so close to Tamara that she could place her cheek against his head if she wanted to.

Standing up, he smiled down on his granddaughter. "You be a good girl."

"I'll try."

He didn't meet Tamara's gaze again before he left. But she did hear him go into the kitchen and say goodbye to her mother, and her responding words.

"Nick, thank you for everything you did today. I don't know what I would have done without you."

****

Nick hadn't contacted Tamara again after spending the day with her daughter though Tamara thought a talk was overdue. She dreaded it because of the secret she kept from him.

Was it wrong not to tell him she was pregnant?

He was the father after all.

But no more a father than his son had been to Miranda. Nick didn't know it, but he had acted as a sperm donor. He had not agreed to parenthood, and she would not, absolutely would not, thrust that role on him. He'd wanted to use protection the night they'd been together. Tamara had refused. She had told him birth control wasn't an issue for her.

He had thought she meant she couldn't get pregnant.

But that wasn't what she'd meant.

She had meant she didn't want to prevent a pregnancy if one happened.

She wanted a baby, and at the time of the baby's conception, Tamara hadn't been sure Nick would be willing to help. She'd acted on the chance that if she got pregnant, the baby's cord blood could cure Miranda.

And besides, Tamara's mother had become pregnant

with her, and Tamara's father had not been happy about it. He had married Sandy, but he'd felt trapped. He'd resented his wife and daughter on up to the day he walked out on them when Tamara was thirteen years old. There was no way Tamara would repeat the mistakes her mother and father had made.

She'd made a decision the night in Atlanta to take a chance, once again, to become a single parent.

It was her sole burden. No one else's.

Charlotte stopped by the house a few days later after work. She walked through the back door without knocking, a practice she'd had for years. Tamara heard the refrigerator door open and close as her friend put in the bottle of wine to chill she'd brought with her, a practice she'd also had for years. She walked into the den where Sandy, Tamara, and Miranda sat.

"Hi, everyone. Thought I'd come by and see how things were going."

"Chocolate!" Miranda stood and ran to her, hugging her around her legs.

"Hey, girlie." Charlotte picked the little girl up. "Wow, that is some cool hair."

"Nicky gave it to me."

She looked at the two women in the room. "Who's Nicky?"

Tamara didn't answer, though she noticed Charlotte's eyes narrowed when she looked at her.

"Nicky is Miranda's grandfather," Sandy supplied.

"Really?" The tone invited an explanation.

"Really," Miranda said. "And he gave me a bunch of wigs and hats, and he even came to stay with me when I had to go to the hospital to get blood in my straw."

Charlotte's mouth opened in shock. "What the heck? I don't call you for two weeks, and Atlas shrugs?"

Tamara still didn't speak. Charlotte stared at her a few more seconds then turned her attention to the little girl in her arms.

"I am loving the blue hair, child. It is beautiful, and the tiara is perfect."

"What's a tiara?"

"It's your diamond crown."

"Oh. What's it called again?"

"A tiara."

"This is my Super Cooper hair and tee-aww-rah. Tee-aww-ruh."

"Tiara."

"Tiara."

"You got it, chickie."

"Want to eat supper with us, Charlotte?" Sandy asked.

"Would love to. I thought this is one of your last nights to be home, isn't it Tamara?"

"Tomorrow night is my last night off, then I switch to second shift. Four in the afternoon to midnight."

"Mama, can I call Nicky and tell him I have a tiara?"

"Not right now. Why don't you show Chocolate your other hats?" Tamara found distracting her daughter when she asked to see or talk to Nick worked most of the time.

Charlotte walked through the room to the treehouse to see Miranda's collection of headwear. But the look Charlotte cast Tamara's way as she went promised that her friend was not going to be as easily dissuaded.

After supper when Miranda had been put to bed and Sandy had retired downstairs, the two friends sat in the den. Charlotte took a sip of wine and set the glass on the coffee table then settled back against the couch.

"Ready to tell me?" she said.

"Tell you what?"

"What's going on?"

Tamara reached under her glasses and rubbed her eyes. "He got tested, and he's not a match."

"Everything you went through to find him, and then… I'm so sorry, Tamara."

"Thanks."

"What's next?"

"She's getting the chemo. That's all we can do right now."

"So, how does Nicolaus Pack fit into all of this? I can't believe you let him meet her."

"He insisted. Against my better judgment, I let it happen."

"So, what? She's got a grandpa now?"

"No. He cannot be a part of our lives."

Charlotte picked up her glass and swirled the liquid inside it. She sipped, watching Tamara the entire time.

"There's something you're not telling me."

"You know the kind of person he is. I don't want him in our lives."

Charlotte crooked her head, still studying her friend. "I found him to be charming, albeit aloof and above the debauchery typical of the conference we attended."

Tamara turned away from her friend's assessing stare.

"What happened between you and him in Atlanta? You never did tell me."

"Nothing."

Charlotte snorted.

Tamara finally turned back to her friend, attempting to return her stare without flinching.

"If you decided I had a pretty good idea after all, and you did the dirty with him—"

"Charlotte—"

"Stay with me now, if you did, and if you and he did, and if that resulted in the reason you are not imbibing with me on this bottle of wine I always bring to share when I eat supper here, then I'd certainly like to know."

"Do you know how slim the chances are that a one time encounter would result in pregnancy in a woman over forty?"

Charlotte clapped her hands in triumph. "I knew it! I knew it! You are!"

"I never said any such thing."

"You did. You said the P word. You are, aren't you?"

Tamara stood up. "I'm not having this conversation with

you." She left the room and walked into the kitchen.

She wasn't ready. She wasn't ready to tell anyone. And as much as she loved Charlotte, the woman was impetuous, and she wasn't that great at keeping secrets.

Taking a few deep breaths, she poured herself a glass of milk and drank. This would be another indicator to Charlotte that she was pregnant. But milk was good for her and the baby. She finished the glass then went back into the den and sat down.

"Want to watch a movie?"

"Aww, come on."

Tamara shook her head. "I'm not discussing it, and you better not tell my mom. I'll tell her when I know for sure it's viable."

Charlotte's eyes widened. "Do you mean it may not be?"

"After twelve weeks, it ought to be, but this is it. This topic is finished."

"What about Nick?"

"What about him?"

"It's his, right? Man! I can't believe you did it with him. I'm impressed. I swear, I didn't think you had it in you."

"No, it isn't his."

"Then whose?"

"Stop it. Discussion is over."

Charlotte leaned forward. "You didn't go to the sperm bank again. I know you didn't."

"Drop it, or leave."

She stuck her tongue out. "Fine. I'm dropping it. For now, but that's something you aren't going to be able to hide forever, you know. When a new baby shows up here, Sandy is going to get suspicious."

"Get out. Charlotte."

Chapter Ten

Tamara sat at the physician's desk and typed in chart notes on a patient who had seventeen new stitches in his hand after an accident with his pocketknife. Her cell phone sat next to the keyboard. She wanted to keep it close because last night Miranda had a meltdown stemming from Tamara's new work schedule.

Accustomed to her mother tucking her in each night, Miranda had cried herself to sleep because Tamara hadn't been home. Even a video chat didn't satisfy her. Tamara had lain down and taken a nap with her this afternoon in the hopes that it could be their new routine.

When her phone screen lit up with Nick's name, Tamara stared at it for a few seconds. He hadn't contacted her since the day Miranda had gotten a pint of blood. Why was he calling now?

She slid her finger across the screen and answered it.

"Dr. Wallace."

"It's Nick."

"What do you want?"

"Miranda just called me. She wants me to come tuck her in. I'm calling to ask permission."

"How did she call you?" Tamara had insisted that Sandy was not to contact him again. No matter what.

"I gave Sandy my number when I came for breakfast. I think Miranda used Sandy's phone without Sandy knowing."

"She did not. Please don't lie to me, Nick. It's demeaning to both of us."

"Miranda's used your phone before to call me. Twice now."

"No, she hasn't."

"Really? Look at your call history. She called me at six thirty the morning of the eighteenth and again last week at two in the afternoon."

"You're wrong. She knows her letters, but she can't read. How could she possibly...." Tamara's voice trailed off. She remembered Nick's name written on the board in the treehouse in Miranda's scrawl. "I'll call you back." She hung up and searched through her phone for the phone call Nick mentioned, and sure enough, there it was. A call made from her phone to Nick's phone the morning Nick had said. The second call was when Tamara had been napping. She thought Miranda had been napping with her.

Oh, Miranda. You're too smart for your mommy.

Tamara called her mother's cell phone. Miranda answered the phone.

"Hey," she said, her usual way of answering the telephone.

"Miranda."

"Hi, Mommy. Can you come home? I miss you." The little girl's voice wobbled.

"I miss you, too, sweetheart, but I can't come home right now. Where's Meemee?"

"She's over there. Can Nicky come see me? I wouldn't miss you so bad if he could come."

"Let me talk to Meemee."

"I *am* trying to sleep, but it's hard."

"Give her the phone. Go and take it to her."

Tamara heard little footfalls and Miranda's breath as she went through the house. "Meemee, Mommy wants to talk to you."

"Hello."

"How is she?"

"She seems better tonight. Went right to bed without any fuss."

"She took your phone with her and called Nick."

"Huh. What a smart little girl."

"Mom, don't encourage that behavior."

Miranda's voice reached her. "Ask Mommy if Nicky can come over tonight. Please? Please, Meemee? He can, can't he?"

"No, Miranda. He can't come over tonight," Sandy said.

"Oh, please, Meemee. Please."

Trauma alert. Fourteen minutes by ground, the alert sounded, and Tamara's beeper sounded. "Mom, I've got to go. I'll try to call later."

Tamara hung up and dialed Nick. He picked up on the first ring. "Why are you talking to her without my knowledge?"

"She just asks if I can come see her. The first time I told her, I'd talk to you about it. The second time, I said I couldn't. But I was very gentle with her. I want to abide by your wishes, but, Tamara, she was crying tonight. I want your permission to go."

"It's not good for her."

"It's not good for her now. Isn't it stressful enough for her that you're not with her at night? Without you keeping me away from her when she wants to see me?"

"I have to work nights right now. You have no right to criticize me."

"Look." He sighed. "You say this is a vulnerable time for her. Okay. Let me spend some time with her until she's done with the chemotherapy. After she finishes, she'll be stronger, right?"

"If the cancer goes into remission." Tamara's voice broke on the last word and she cleared her throat.

"The chemo will work, and the cancer will go into remission. Let's assume that. Afterward, you and I will make a plan to ease me out of her life. But right now, she seems to need me, and I don't mind. I want to do this for her."

Tamara bowed her head and rubbed her temple with one hand. "You don't know what you're getting into."

Ten minutes before the trauma arrived.

"Let me spend some time with her just until she goes into remission."

"She may not go into remission," Tamara whispered.

"Don't say that. She is going to get better, dammit."

"You don't know. You don't know how serious this disease is." She glanced at the clock. She needed to pull herself together.

"I think I do know. Let me make tonight better for her." When Tamara didn't say anything, he continued. "Please, Tamara."

The months of bearing the burden of the cancer weighed heavy on Tamara. The suspicion of what it could be before the diagnosis was confirmed. Putting on the brave doctor face to every person when her mother's heart screamed and wailed in helplessness. Encouraging Miranda to eat, to drink, to suffer through another needle stick, another pill to swallow, another infusion through the "straw", to do every single thing a four-year-old shouldn't have to do when the chasm of fear threatened to swallow Tamara.

"I know what it's like to lose a child. I can understand your fear because I've lived it. Tamara, let me do this for Miranda."

Something broke in Tamara's defenses. Maybe it was because she was so tired of trying to be brave for everyone else. Maybe it was because Nick recognized her fear for what it was. He recognized it, and wanted to help.

"Okay."

Tamara was late leaving the hospital. When she pulled her car into the driveway, it was nearly two in the morning. Nick's car was parked in front of the house. Why was he still here? Was something wrong? She entered through the kitchen door, and walked into the den. Where was he? She went upstairs, peeking into Miranda's room on her way to her own. The nightlight illuminated Nick slumbering on the single bed where Tamara usually slept.

He must have fallen asleep.

Tamara went to her private bathroom and took a shower, then slipped into a long T-shirt and pair of pajama pants. She padded into Miranda's room, bent down felt her forehead and her cheek, then kissed her. The whisper of movement on a bedded sheet reached her ears. When she turned, Nick sat on the edge of the bed.

He rubbed his face. "I guess I fell asleep."

"I guess you came here after all."

"Yes. I started out in the rocking chair. She fell asleep, or so I thought, but when I stood up to leave, she asked me where I was going."

"You could have told her it was time for you to go."

"I did. She said she didn't want me to."

"My mom could have sat with her."

"I didn't mind, but after a while, the bed looked inviting, so I thought I'd lie down until you got home."

Tamara took two steps toward him. Gratitude for what he had done tonight drowned out the misgivings she had about him becoming involved in Miranda's life. "Thank you."

He gazed at her for a moment, as if he had detected the shift in her feelings. "Come sit down for a minute. You must be tired."

Tamara yawned, but otherwise didn't move.

"Come on. You've had a hard night, I bet." He patted the spot next to him.

"I usually sleep here," she said, taking the few steps it took to reach the bed.

Nick reached up and grasped her hand then tugged. "So, you can watch her at night."

"Yes."

"You smell good."

"I take a shower first thing when I get home. I want to be sure I don't bring any germs from the ER."

She felt Nick's hand behind her neck. She tensed.

"It's all right. I'm not going to bite you," he murmured. His fingers pressed into the muscles between her neck and shoulder, kneading them.

"You should go home," she whispered.

"I will."

The heat of his body drew her, and in spite of herself,

she leaned against him. The massage felt so good on her fatigued flesh.

"I'm tired."

"I know you are. Why don't you lie down?"

It seemed like a reasonable suggestion. Tamara moved her legs and scooted on the other side of his body. She reclined on the bed, then lay on her side. He shifted and moved closer to the foot of the bed.

She looked up at him, and he met her gaze. "You'll let yourself out, right?"

"Yes." But instead of standing and leaving, Nick lay down, too, turning toward her though he didn't embrace her. With only a couple of inches in between them in the small bed, he reached and took her hand, interlacing his fingers with hers. Tamara wanted to ask him why he wasn't leaving, but her eye lids felt so heavy. She closed them and felt his thumb caress her hand. It was the last sensation Tamara had before she fell asleep.

When she awoke the next morning with a start, Nick was gone. But his scent lingered on the pillow.

Instead of the self-recrimination Tamara expected, she only felt a tenderness for a man who would drive an hour to comfort a little girl, then hold hands with the girl's mom while she fell asleep after a long night at work.

What was happening here?

Tamara turned and saw Miranda was gone from her bed. Tamara took the pillow, bunched it, and inhaled.

Nick, what are you doing to me?

"Good morning, how was work?" Sandy's voice brought Tamara's face out of the pillow.

Sandy held two cups of coffee and offered one to her. Tamara looked at it, debating about whether to drink it or not. Coffee really wasn't good for the baby.

"Don't you want it?"

Tamara sat up. She scooted back against the wall. "There's something I need to tell you."

"All right."

"This is a biggie. You better sit down."

Sandy sat next to her on the bed and waited.

"I'm pregnant."

The older woman's mouth fell open. "You're what?"

"Pregnant. I'm hoping the baby will be a match so we can use the cord blood for Miranda."

Sandy put her hand to her chest. "Nick."

"Please, Mom. Don't."

She turned stricken eyes to her daughter. "He's not the father?"

"When I was in Atlanta, I obtained a sperm donor."

"Why did you go all the way to Atlanta for that? I thought you went to talk to Nick."

"I did. I did get to talk to him while I was down there, but he doesn't know anything about this, so please don't say a word about it."

"I thought you were going to go to the clinic here. What happened?"

"I had a connection there. It looked like it could be a good match, so I did it. I didn't tell you until now because I wasn't sure it would work, but the doctor says everything looks really good."

"My heavens. I'm just so shocked."

"This is a good thing, Mom. I didn't think I would be able to get pregnant with just one try, but I have, and Miranda will have a little brother or sister. It will be so good for all of us."

Sandy nodded. "We'll need to go shopping."

****

Good morning.

Tamara stared at the words on her cell phone screen from Nick. She didn't know how to respond. What should she say?

Good morning.

When did you leave?

You're going to be a father again.

Will you hate me for that?

None of those responses seemed good. Then another text from him.

Sandy says Miranda has chemo today. Do you need any help?

Ah. Now there was something safe to text about.

Her daughter's cancer and chemo treatment.

Tamara tapped on the screen.

No help needed today. She will likely sleep for the rest of the day after treatment.

Why? He texted back.

Medicine given with chemo to prevent an allergic reaction makes her sleepy.

I could come over tomorrow night.

He was offering to help out tomorrow night. Miranda would likely be very clingy because the chemo made her tired and weak. At least, she had been the other times. Tamara had always been able to be home in the evenings at bedtime, when routine and snuggling were most important.

Mom could handle it, certainly.

Will get back to you, she texted him.

Tamara tucked her phone in her pocket and walked through the house. She'd been in her home office paying bills at the computer when Nick's text had come through. Their appointment for the infusion therapy wasn't for an hour and a half. Sounds from the treehouse sent Tamara upstairs where Sandy and Miranda were playing Candy Land on the floor.

Miranda's blue green hair tilted back when the little girl looked up at her. "Want to play, Mommy?"

"Sure."

"Got a text for you, Meemee," Tamara told her mom, a code for them when they wanted to share a message without Miranda hearing.

"My phone is downstairs. Let me see yours."

Tamara opened the notepad and typed on it:

Nick offered to come over tomorrow night. Do you want help? She handed the phone over the board game to her mother.

"If you start now, Mommy, you're going to be behind."

"That's okay." She drew a card with a colored square on

it and moved her gingerbread man forward.

Sandy read the message and arched an eyebrow. Her finger moved across the screen and she handed it back to her daughter.

Would love for Nick to come over.

Tamara looked from her phone screen to her mother who watched her steadily.

She typed. *Do not say anything about the baby* and gave it back.

I won't but maybe he wouldn't mind.

"What?" Tamara asked.

Again, her eyebrow arched, and this time Sandy smiled. "He's very attractive."

"Who? King Candy?" Miranda asked.

"Isn't he a little young for you?" Tamara asked her mother.

"Yes, much too young for me. But not for you." Sandy picked up a card from the deck and pushed her game piece up two purple spaces.

"Umm, no."

"If you would just give him a chance. Can't you see how much he wants to be in her life? And now with..."

Tamara glared at Sandy, and she didn't finish her sentence.

"Your turn, Meemee," Miranda said.

Tamara shifted her legs on the floor. "Yes, I see how he is with her, but it isn't about me. She reminds him of the son he lost."

"It's more than that. I can tell." Sandy took her turn on the board.

Tamara studied the colorful game instead of meeting the gaze of her mother. "I can't get into this right now."

"He's not married. I already asked him."

Tamara picked the top card and looked at the picture of molasses. "Lovely."

"Who's not married, Meemee?" Miranda wanted to know, then her eyes widened when Tamara laid down the card she'd drawn. "Oh, Mommy. You're in trouble. You're going to get stuck in Molasses Swamp."

"She's stuck, all right," Sandy commented.

"Only for one turn, Meemee." Tamara drew another card. It was the Cupcake which put her back down close to the starting point.

"Hey! You got two candies in a row!" Miranda clapped her hands. In her mind, getting to land on the candy spaces was special no matter where they were on the board.

"It must be your lucky day, Tamara." Sandy smiled.

Tamara wished that was the case, but it wasn't.

As expected, Miranda pitched a fit when they arrived at the hospital. She screamed and cried so much in the waiting room that Tamara had to take her out to the parking lot until they called her back to the room for the infusion. In consultation with the doctor, he and Tamara decided to give Miranda a mild sedative. And in a few minutes, the child had calmed enough for the nurse to connect the chemo to the PICC line below Miranda's collarbone.

After the treatment, Sandy drove home with Miranda, and Tamara went to the emergency department. She called Nick, thinking to leave a message, but he picked up.

"How'd it go?" he asked.

"She doesn't like coming to the hospital. Every time is a battle. I would have thought by now she'd be used to it."

"I'm sorry it's so difficult."

"Me too. I wish I could make her understand this medicine is helping her."

"It's hard to see your kid get so upset and not be able to make it better. It's a damn helpless feeling."

Tamara sat back in the doctor's lounge where she'd gone for respite before her shift started. She took off her glasses and rubbed the bridge of her nose. "Yes, it is."

"I'll try to take off a little early tomorrow. Maybe spend some time with her before she has to go to sleep."

"She'll still be pretty tired."

"So, no swimming or relay races?"

Tamara smiled. "If she's up to it, sure. And you don't have to wait until I get home to leave. Mom doesn't tend to stay in her room with her, but we both have baby monitors in our bedrooms, so Mom can hear from downstairs if Miranda needs her."

"Then why do you sleep in Miranda's room if you've got a monitor?"

"Because she's my baby. I rest better when I can see her. I can hear her with the monitor, but being close by, it just helps me to know."

"I understand."

Chapter Eleven

The following night, Nick's car was in the driveway when Tamara arrived home. She took her shower and sorted through her shirts and pajama bottoms trying to find the least worn out and stretched out pair. What did it matter anyway? Was she trying to impress Nick? Would he even notice? Her hand touched silk, and Tamara pulled out a pajama set Charlotte had given her for her birthday one year. They were black trimmed in red on the seams. Charlotte had dared her to wear them in place of her scrubs at work.

"If you're going to wear pajamas to work, black is much more slimming," she'd said with a sparkle in her eyes.

Did Tamara dare wear these in the other room?

What would Nick think?

Silly.

Tamara put them back in the drawer and picked up her Duke T-shirt. She put one arm in the sleeve and paused.

She remembered his expression next to the bed in the hotel room as he gazed down upon her, making her feel that she was the most beautiful woman on the planet.

Tamara wouldn't mind seeing that look again.

In fact, she needed a dose of that look.

She tossed aside the T-shirt and walked over to her underwear drawer. Charlotte had given her some black panties and a demi-bra as well. Nick may not see what was under her black pajamas tonight, but wearing the pretty lingerie would give Tamara a little more confidence. She hadn't been ready to seduce him when she'd flown down to Atlanta, but she'd bedded him anyway.

Maybe this time, she could relax knowing he knew who she was.

Just what the doctor ordered.

Tamara filled her lungs with a fortifying breath and took determined steps out of her bedroom into her daughter's room. The pajamas didn't have to mean anything. They weren't indecent. Sure, there was a little lace on the front, but she wouldn't be embarrassed to wear them in the house. Nick probably wouldn't even notice.

Tamara padded into Miranda's room and saw Nick was sitting in the rocking chair reading from a thick bound notebook and beneath the notebook, was Gary the cat.

Tamara suppressed a smile.

Nick looked up as she entered. Tamara nodded a greeting as she approached Miranda's sleeping form on the bed. Tamara bent down and placed her cheek on her daughter's forehead, feeling of her skin. She inhaled her daughter's sweet not quite baby scent and carefully removed the wig.

Placing the wig on the dresser, she moved back to her daughter and kissed the scalp she had exposed and tucked the covers securely around her shoulders. Miranda sighed in her sleep but otherwise didn't move. Tamara watched her for a moment before she turned toward Nick. He had placed the book on the floor next to the chair, and one hand petted Gary whose tail flitted back and forth.

"You and Gary made friends, huh?"

"He kept getting on the bed with Miranda. I was afraid he'd try to lay on top of her."

"Cats stealing children's breath is a wives' tale."

"He weighs fifteen pounds, at least. If he gets on her, as he attempted to several times, she will have trouble breathing."

Nick's concern warmed Tamara.

"Your cat needs to be on a diet." He scratched the cat behind the ears as if showing he was teasing.

"How did Miranda do tonight?"

"Seemed fatigued. She sat next to me on the couch the whole time. She didn't even want to go to the table to eat.

But Sandy took it in stride and brought dinner to her."

"Did she eat anything?"

"A few bites, and that was with me pouring all of my charm into convincing her."

Tamara surmised his charm would be hard to resist. "Thank you for coming over. You can go home now."

Gary jumped to the floor with a disgruntled meow, and Nick stood. "You expect me to leave when you're wearing that?"

Heat crawled up Tamara's chest until she thought her face would burst into flames. *Oh, how stupid of me. Why did I think this was a good idea?* She pushed her glasses up to the bridge of her nose and strode toward the door.

"Where are you going?"

"To change clothes," she said.

"Please don't."

Tamara paused at the threshold, unsure what to do. Was he flirting with her? Sincere? Men didn't speak to her this way, so she had no experience on which to base an appropriate response.

She heard his footsteps approach her, and she held her breath.

"May I touch you?" he asked.

Yes! No! Tamara didn't know what to say.

"Tamara?"

The way he spoke her name made butterflies flutter in her stomach. It was the same way he'd spoken her name when he'd made love to her. When he thought her name was Tomorrow. "What?"

"Will you turn around and look at me?"

Will I? Yes, I can do that. Tamara turned around and looked up at Nick who stood in front of her now. The room was lit only with the low lamp near the rocking chair. It meant Nick's face was in shadow. "You're lovely," he murmured.

"Don't."

"Don't what?"

"Don't say things like that."

"Why not?"

"It makes me uncomfortable."

Nick lips turned up in a smile. She could see that much at least. She remembered what those lips had felt like on her mouth, her skin, her....

"Why is that, do you think? Because of our night in Atlanta?"

"How am I supposed to respond to that?"

"With the truth, I hope."

Fear that somehow he had found out about the baby caused Tamara to search his face for an expression of anger or regret.

"If you could go back and relive that night, would you do anything different?"

"I don't see the relevance of playing what-if games, Nick."

"Maybe you don't, but I do." Nick's fingers splayed on her upper arms. He ran his hands up to her shoulders and back down to her elbows. "If I could have a do over, I wouldn't leave you. I would have crawled back in bed with you and loved you for the rest of the night. I would have kissed away the tears falling from your eyes and beg you to tell me what I did to elicit them. I would have held you until dawn or until you knew you could trust me enough to tell me you were the mother of my grandchild, and that you had flown all the way down there to do whatever it took to save your daughter's life, even making love to the son of a bitch who blew you off outside of his office that day weeks before."

Tamara grasped his arm and turning, she pulled him out of the room, down the hall, and to her bedroom. Pausing long enough to shut the door, she dropped her hand and reached down to turn on the baby monitor on her bedside table. She crossed her arms over her chest.

"I'd rather you not do that in there. Miranda does tend to be a heavy sleeper, but people can still hear while sleeping, and she is no exception."

"I'm sorry."

"She can't know. She can't ever know that I would.... That I would do what I did."

"Because of her."

"Whatever my reasons, I'd rather her not know I would trick a man into having sex with me. She wouldn't understand it now, but one day she might decide the behavior was inappropriate and be ashamed of me. I don't want that."

"You didn't trick me into anything. Your only crime was not telling me who you were or why you were there. I am responsible for my actions that night. You continue to withhold information. Why did you do it?"

Tamara shook her head slowly.

Nick watched her, and she returned his stare. "I thought you were going to blackmail me into giving the marrow, but you knew in Atlanta I was already considering doing it, and you seemed almost apologetic when you came to my office afterward. So, no, I don't think that was ever your intention. Even as desperate as I know you were, you wouldn't stoop to that." He'd ended the sentence with an inquisitive tone, as if still trying to gage if she would or not.

"You might be surprised at what I'm capable of doing if it meant Miranda could live."

"Anything."

"Most anything. My own life, certainly."

"If there were another donor located. Another person who was a match, you would move heaven and earth to get the marrow. Is that right?"

"It would depend if the donor's life would be compromised in the process. I would rather not be put in the position to decide. As the mother of the recipient, I couldn't be objective."

"If you were the mother of the donor, the parent of the donor, you would get to decide though."

Fear rose in her chest. He knew. Somehow he had figured out what she'd done.

"If that donor was still underage. Then the parent decides. As a doctor, what would your recommendation be?"

Tamara stepped backward. "I'm... I can't be objective."

Nick inched toward her. "The very fact that you acknowledge it makes me think you can be amazingly objective."

"It's late. You should leave."

His eyes burned into hers. "Would you? Let's say it was another child, and Miranda was older. She was healthy, would you give permission for her to donate if she were a match?"

He knew. He knew about the baby. "Are you playing games with me?"

He shook his head. "No. I just want us to be honest with each other, and I want you to...."

"No. Please, Nick. I can't talk about that anymore. About possible donors or matches, if that's what you're getting at."

"Okay. I just have another question... or two."

Tamara held her breath.

Nick raised his hand and scratched his chin reflectively. "Was Atlanta just an act? You seemed so...open. Now, any time I try to connect, you put these walls up. I understand that Miranda is sick, and most of your focus needs to be on her, but I think it's more than that. I think it has to do with Atlanta. Is it because I hurt you that night?"

"No," she breathed.

"I shouldn't have left. That was a mistake. It was all a lot more intense than I expected." He moved forward a few steps more.

"What's your other question?"

"If you won't tell me why you slept with me, will you at least tell me why you were crying?" He was in front of her now. Gentleness showing in his eyes. Trust me, they expressed.

Maybe he didn't know about the baby after all. Maybe Tamara's guilt made her imagine things. "It's hard to admit."

"Tell me."

"You know when I told you about being allergic to latex?" He nodded, and Tamara continued. "I know because when I was in college my boyfriend and I were having intercourse, and I went into anaphylaxis. He called 911, and I went to the hospital. That's the only time I've ever had sex until with you."

A shocked expression ran across his face.

"My first sexual encounter was rather brief because of the physiological reaction to the latex. I was afraid and ashamed. Embarrassed, certainly. Needless to say, I carry some emotional baggage from that night. You were...." Tamara paused. "You made me feel very beautiful and sexy that night. I appreciate it more than you know."

"Then why are you so hesitant to let me get close to you, to Miranda? Is it because of how I acted when you first met me?"

Tamara dropped her eyes. Nick stood in front of her now, almost touching her. He picked up her hands and held them in his. His thumb grazed back and forth over her skin. She shivered. She sensed him lowering his head. *He's going to kiss me.*

"Tamara. I'm sorry. I'm so sorry."

She still didn't look up at him, focusing instead on his pale green button down shirt, the pearl colored buttons. Nick lifted her right hand. He turned her arm and opened her palm and placed his lips on her wrist and another and another, marking a trail up her forearm.

She wanted to tell him, but she was afraid. If she told him she'd had unprotected sex with him knowing she could get pregnant, he'd be angry. She'd told him birth control wasn't an issue though she knew her cycle well enough to realize she could conceive, and she had. She'd misled him. She had a good reason to. The cord blood could be used to cure Miranda if the baby was a match. It was a long shot, but at the time, she really didn't know if Nick was going to help her.

He placed her hand on his chest and slid his arm around

her, moving closer still.

"Will you forgive me?" he whispered, his mouth descended and touched hers. "Please forgive me."

"If you'll forgive me," she whispered back against his lips and returned his kiss. His face knocked her glasses, and she dropped her head back, removed the glasses and placed them on the night stand. Nick's face became a cottony soft image. Tamara could no longer see the expression in his eyes or the cleft above his lip. She closed her eyes, and breathed in. The husky scent of whatever cologne he wore teased her nostrils. And the heat from his body and arms cocooned her in, making her feel safe and cherished.

I'm so sorry I misled you, that you didn't get a say about the baby.
He brushed his lips back and forth over hers.

"You can put your tongue in my mouth," he murmured.

Excitement and fear sparked all the nerve endings in her body.

He held her hand still at his chest.

"Do you think it's disgusting? Is that why you won't?"

Tamara shook her head. "I'm not good at this. I've never…." She huffed and would have pulled away, but Nick held her.

"You're damn good at this. Taste me, Tamara." He opened her fisted hand and guided it down his chest to his stomach and up again. "Touch me. Whatever you want to do, I want you to." He nuzzled her cheek and rained kisses along her jaw until he stopped at the corner of her mouth. "Do you want to?"

"Yes." She moved her face a fraction of an inch and met his lips, pliant and still. He waited on her to kiss him, taste him. She nudged her tongue across his lower lip and dipped it across the barrier. His mouth opened a fraction more. Tamara ventured farther encountering his own tongue. She moved within him as he had done to her, discovering the taste and texture of this man who had explored her body so thoroughly weeks ago. He growled appreciatively, and the sound encouraged her to stroke the inner recesses of his mouth.

Tamara had been the passive participant with Nick before, but now he invited her to take charge, to initiate and seek. Her fingers nimbly unbuttoned his shirt, pulling it free of his slacks. When she freed the last button, he shrugged out of it hurriedly without breaking contact with her lips. She heard the sound of the shirt landing on the floor. He wore an undershirt, the soft cotton bunched under her hand as she sought the feel of his bare skin beneath. He was soft and firm together, his muscles rippling against her questing fingertips.

Tamara dipped her head, and lifting the material further, she kissed his chest licking the flesh there, and when she closed her lips over his nipple, his whole body shuddered.

"Tamara," he said feverishly.

Leaning back, she attempted to see the expression on his face, but couldn't. She wanted to continue undressing him, but hesitated. It was such a bold move, and Nick didn't strike her as timid.

Not in any way.

Maybe he didn't want a woman doing something so wanton, so reckless.

"I can't see you without my glasses. I can't read you."

"Sure, you can." He moved his hands over her backside and nudged her closer to his body. She felt heat and something stiff pressing against her, and realized with a burst of power, he was erect.

I'm responsible for that.

"Have you been with anyone since you were with me?"

"No, Tamara. No one since you."

She watched the gauzy features of his face as she reached forward and felt his belt. The metallic click of the buckle as she loosened it accompanied the tingling of her thighs, as if her body knew the sound meant soon the desire building there would be addressed.

Indulged.

Savored.

Consumed.

She grasped the buckle and pulled, hearing the slick rasp of leather slipping through loops. Tamara held the belt up with one outstretched arm and dropped it.

The Monet mouth lifted in a smile.

She freed the button and in the quiet of the room, the zipper released its clasping teeth, a soundtrack to the yearning building like a Tsunami inside her.

Her hand skimmed him before scaling northward to his stomach, her finger tracing a lazy circle around his navel. Nick shoved his shirt up and off. It, too, landed on the floor. Tamara leaned forward and licked and nipped his skin enjoying the revealed landscape. Pulling at her front alerted her that Nick was releasing the buttons on her shirt. He wrenched the black satin apart, then his hands cupped her breasts. When his palms covered her nipples with only the wispy material of her bra separating flesh from flesh, Tamara gasped.

She grasped his head and pulled his face to her chest.

He peeled her shirt and bra straps over the curve of her shoulders, and his mouth closed over one breast through the fabric of the undergarment. Reaching behind her, she attempted to unhook the clasp. The movement arched her body forward into Nick. With one hand, he uncovered her breast and with the other he moved over her fingers to aid her.

The eyehooks released, the binding of the bra was gone. Completely gone. The relief of the restriction overcame her, and she pivoted and stepped, moving Nick to back up until his legs pressed against the bed and he sat down hard. She stood in front of him, his knees bookending her legs.

His face tilted upward as if he watched her when he ensconced the tip of her breast with his lips leisurely before laving the skin beneath. Inching her pants down her hips, he followed the progress of his hands licking a trail across her stomach and placed his mouth over her hip bone jutting out and sucked the skin hard.

Needed him. She needed him inside her now. Right now.

His big hands circled her thigh, one thumb easing into her. The contact so explosive, she bit down on her lip and dug her fingernails into his shoulders.

"You like that, do you?"

His fingers delved deeper, and already a wonderful urgent feeling spiraled upward.

Now. Now.

Tamara pushed him down on the bed and climbed over him, bending over and frantically seeking to bring her lips to his and shoving his pants off. In a few chaotic seconds, he'd lost his pants, and Tamara kicked hers free. She knelt, fitted him into her, and rocked steadily trying to keep control but losing it until it seemed the whole world was tilting crazily.

A kaleidoscope of energy rocketed outward, and she rode the wave vaguely aware that Nick's body tensed under hers and for a few delicious eternities, his arms banded around her tightly even as their sweat-slicked bodies careened against each other. She wanted to hang onto that marvelous sensation, but in a nuclear flash, it was gone, and she was floating languorously down. She stilled, trying to catch her breath.

Oh, my gosh. Oh, my gosh.

So, that's what an orgasm felt like.

Sensations returned to her. Nick's arms still around her, his breathing, too, labored. She began to move off him.

His arms tightened. "Where are you going?" he growled.

"Moving so I don't smother you."

"Stay here. Right here. Smother me."

Tamara raised her head and looked down at him. Her hair partially covered his face, and she stretched her neck and smoothed the locks away tucking them behind her shoulder.

"Why did you do that? I like your hair."

"You like my hair in your face," she said in disbelief.

"Yes, all over my face. All over me." Nick reached up with his hands and tangled his fingers through it. "I've never felt hair so beautifully curly, like burnished gold ringlets."

In spite of what he said, Tamara slid off him and picked

up her glasses. She slipped them on her face and peered at him. He had several strands in his fingers moving it out and letting it spring back in its curls.

His jaw and chin shadowed with nearly a days' growth of beard. Miranda's body prickled at the memory of the rough skin rubbing against hers.

"Miranda's hair is curly, isn't it?"

Tamara watched his full lips form the words. She wanted those lips on hers again. On every part of her. "Yes."

"It'd have to be. Reggie's hair was curly. He hated it."

She remembered the detailed survey she'd read. The one she'd chosen as the biological father of her child. "His curly hair was one of the reasons I chose him. That and he had red hair. I also liked that he was musical."

"Musical." Nick laughed. Tamara felt his chuckles against her body. She rested her chin on her hand resting on his chest.

"What?" It was strange and wonderful. They were completely nude, and Tamara's leg intertwined with his.

Didn't he realize how significant this was? They'd made love in Tamara's bedroom. She'd had the best—the very best—sex in her whole life. And they lay here as if they'd been together for decades.

"He played drums in middle and high school," Nick said, the amusement evident in his voice.

"The drums?"

"And every time he stayed at my house, he bugged the hell out of me because he always had his music on." Nick's hand moved over Tamara's bottom, moving over the flesh, lightly squeezing it. The intimacy of the gesture made her heart turn over. "But a musician? I think he was stretching the truth."

Nick was beautiful. Tamara surveyed his body, lying on her bed. Their nudity didn't seem to bother him.

It bothered Tamara. She wished she had her bra back on. Her boobs looked a lot better incased in the pretty black fabric. She decided to tuck her body into his. She moved, repositioning her body.

"What are you doing?" Nick asked.

"I need to go back in Miranda's room soon. Can we cover up for a few minutes until then?"

Nick's arm tightened around her, and he sat up bringing her with him. They moved the sheet and comforter down and settled beneath them with Tamara spooned to his side, her head on his shoulder.

"Better?" he asked spreading her hair over his chest.

Tamara gripped the sheet resting at his hips and began to pull it upward to cover them further.

"Are you cold?"

"No."

Nick laughed softly. He turned and faced her. "You little modest thing." He traced a finger from her shoulder to her breast and tugged the sheet down exposing her breast.

"Stop teasing me."

He bent down and kissed the flesh he'd exposed, and the drifting satiation swelled to yearning.

"No teasing. I'm completely sincere." The intensity in his gaze paralyzed her as he took her breast in his mouth and sucked.

"I wonder if there were other things on the donor survey sheet he wasn't honest about."

Nick raised his head, breaking contact. He sighed and laid his head on her chest, his green gaze turning troubled. "He had problems with drugs. That's why I asked you if a parent using drugs could have caused leukemia in their child."

"They would have tested him extensively. He wasn't using during the time he donated the sperm." Tamara placed her hand on his head and petted his hair. "Is that why you and Reginald were estranged?"

"His mother was an alcoholic. I gave her an ultimatum. Either me or the booze. When I came home from the office the next day, she was gone."

"So, you didn't leave Brenda. Brenda left you."

"Yes. I think Reg blamed me, even though I didn't do

the leaving. Brenda always spun things so that she was the victim, and I tried to get custody, but the judge was a son of a bitch. You'd think he'd put the kids' welfare before the wants of their mother, but in this case, the judge didn't. I tried to get her into rehab so many times. Then one night she called me because Reg had been arrested for a DUI, and she wanted me to make bail for him. But I didn't do it because I thought it would be a good lesson for him. Brenda didn't agree, and I looked like the uncaring father."

"It must have been painful for you to feel so helpless."

"Terrible. I'd like to blame Brenda, but after a while, it just got easier to ignore it all. I was at fault, too." His pained expression tore at Tamara's heart.

"I'm sure you did the best you could at the time."

"I don't know. Reg was our problem child—always testing the limits. He died in stages, I think. I felt like he had been dying for two years before it actually happened. And when I found out, it really didn't hurt that bad, because it was finally over. Except it wasn't because he owed a lot of people money, and they kept showing up, even threatening me at times."

"Is that why you refused to talk to me that day outside of your office? You thought I was a drug dealer?"

"After a while, anyone who mentioned my son's name to me, I just cut off the conversation right then because it generally came around to Reg owing them money. And if they had given a shit about him, instead of their next fix or making sure he had his next fix, maybe he would still be alive today."

Tamara pulled her up to him and wrapped her arms around him. "I'm so sorry it came to that."

He kissed her sweetly, then tucked his face in the curve of her neck. "Meeting you and Miranda, it makes me think there was some redemption when Reg went to the sperm bank." Nick raised up on one elbow and looked down into Tamara's eyes. His own eyes were misty with emotion. "Knowing that part of him went toward creating that little girl in there. She's so precious, Tamara."

"Yes, she is."

Chapter Twelve

Tamara hadn't dated much, but she expected some gesture on Nick's part after their night together. After all, he still wanted to be in Miranda's life. Even if he felt their love making was a mistake, he'd know a way to let Tamara down gently.

She waited a day for word from him, but nothing came. Finally, she texted him.

This is Tamara Wallace.

She hit the send button then wanted to kick herself. Of course, he'd know who she was.

Hello Dr Wallace. This is Nick. How are things at the emergency department at Arm Forks County Hospital?

Trauma day so busy.

Can't get you off my mind.

Her eyebrows rose when she read his words. She was having the same problem.

Her phone rang, and she read Nick's name on the screen. Her heart sped up in excitement and fear. She wasn't ready to talk to him so soon.

"Dr. Wallace," she greeted him.

"What time is your dinner break?"

Tamara laughed. "You must be joking. If I get a break at all, it's certainly not set and I don't have time to go anywhere."

"Not even the cafeteria?"

"Rarely. I'm off Saturday, if you want to come over and see Miranda."

"I'd like to see you, too."

"I'll be there. You can see me."

"Will you wear the black pajamas again?"

"Stop it. I have to go. Just let me know if you want to come over Saturday."

At seven that evening, Crystal, the unit clerk, paged her. Tamara had just finished stitching a lacerated finger. She washed her hands and went to the desk. Two young men stood there with several large brown bags. Their shirts announced they were from the local sandwich deli.

"Did you need me?"

"Tamara Wallace?" one man asked.

"Yes."

"Got your food here. Two sandwich trays and a fruit platter."

"You got dinner for everyone, Dr. Wallace?" Crystal said. "Wow!"

Tamara shook her head at the man. "You're mistaken. I didn't order anything."

He peered at a paper. "Call in. Says here, 'Dinner's on me. Nick'. He took care of the tip and everything."

"Who's Nick?" Crystal asked.

Tamara wasn't sure how to answer the question, so she ignored it. "Come with me. I'll take you to the breakroom." She decided to go ahead and eat now before the staff found out there was free food and devoured it, leaving nothing but the plastic containers and maybe a crumb or two.

****

Syncope.

Tamara washed her hands in the sink located inside of room 5 in the Emergency Department and dried them with the paper towel hanging from the automatic dispenser.

The presenting problem inputted by the triage nurse did not match the patient's blood pressure readings, so Tamara ordered an EKG to rule out any heart issues. She walked to her desk and began charting notes when Crystal, the charge nurse, approached.

"Hi. We've got a frequent flyer in 14. Lenard said he showed up yesterday complaining of chest pains, but left AMA."

Tamara continued typing, but shrugged. "The patient probably got tired of waiting. What's new?"

"Yesterday when he came in, he asked for you by name, and when Lenard said you weren't working, he left."

"Still in pain this afternoon, obviously."

"His arm today. Possible fracture, and he requested you again."

Tamara finished her charting on the syncope patient and stood.

"Obviously, another satisfied customer," she commented. Patients didn't get to request who their ER doctor would be, so either the charge nurse was feeling generous or the patient just got lucky.

Tamara walked by Cole who stood at one of the nurse's stations staring at a computer monitor.

"I'm going to Room 14. That's your patient, right?"

"Yeah." He closed the program, and they walked side by side down the hall. A wide sliding glass door enclosed each room, and a curtain could be drawn across the inside for privacy. This room's curtain was drawn to the side, and the door stood all the way open. Inside a teenager dressed in blue jeans and a ragged yellow T-shirt sat on the edge of the examining table. He looked to be around seventeen years old, and he held his left arm in the other as if he were cradling a baby.

"I'm Dr. Wallace," Tamara said entering the room. She pulled examining gloves from the box on the wall and approached the patient, already studying his arm, which was red and swollen.

"I'm Devon Pack." The last name brought Tamara's attention from the young man's arm to his face. "I think you know my dad, Nicolaus."

Nick had another son, and he hadn't told Tamara. Her gaze roved over the young man, seeking any similar features to confirm his words. The nose, perhaps, and, yes, the same jaw and chin, but his eyes were brown, his hair was a dishwater blond. Tamara stepped beside him, attempting to recover from the shocking news.

"How old are you, Devon?"

"Sixteen."

She gently probed his forearm. "What happened?"

"I fell."

"Fell how?"

"Off a skateboard."

She would have missed his flinch when she moved his arm if she hadn't been paying close attention. "Don't you live in Charleston?" she asked.

"Yes. Haven't you been to my house?" His question wasn't accusatory, only curious.

"No, I haven't." She regarded him. "If you live in Charleston, why are you coming here for medical care?"

His mouth turned up at the corner, and she recognized Nick's smile. "Why do you think?"

Her heart thumped painfully in her chest.

Nick had another son.

"X-ray?" Cole asked.

Tamara shook her head. "He's a minor. We need parental consent."

"Call your father. Tell him he needs to get here now."

"Why don't you call him? You've got his number."

Uneasiness tugged at her. Was Devon fishing for information, or did he know everything? Well, not everything. Even Nick didn't know everything. But what did Devon know? Obviously, he'd known more than she had, since he knew about her.

"On a scale from one to ten, how would you rate your pain?" She pulled out her stethoscope and listened to his heart rate and lungs.

Devon shrugged. "It's not that bad."

"On a scale from one to ten," Tamara repeated.

"If I say ten, do I get some pain pills?"

"No."

"Then I'd say probably a three."

She didn't believe him. His blood pressure was elevated,

and he had perspiration standing on his face. However, his heart rate was within normal parameters.

"Did my dad tell you he had a son? That he had two sons?"

Betrayal shot through her like a lightning bolt. Did Devon mean himself and Reginald, or was there yet another son?

"This is a conversation for another time. My purpose right now is to address your medical issues." Tamara moved away from him, disposed of the gloves, and began washing her hands at the sink. "Cole, make sure his parents are contacted."

"Good luck. Neither one of them are around much these days."

Tamara took a few deep breaths as she methodically dried her hands. "Is your mother living?"

A pause. "No."

So, he was Reginald's full brother, and there wasn't a Mrs. Nicolaus Pack who was his mother.

Tamara crossed her arms over her chest. She studied the young man who still held his arm she was pretty sure was fractured. "I'm sorry. Very sorry for what you've been through. You may not believe this, but I'm glad you came in tonight. When your dad gets here, we'll talk again, okay?"

Relief blanketed his face.

Tamara turned and strode out of the bay. She bypassed the doctor's station and went instead toward the lounge. She heard Cole behind her. Going into the room, she almost made it to the chair when her legs gave way under her.

"Whoa," Cole said when he caught her shoulders. "Easy, Doctor." He guided her to the chair.

"I need to get on the floor. For God's sake, shut and lock the door, will you?" she gasped.

Cole closed the door then helped her to lie down on the floor. She raised her legs and placed her feet on the chair. Elevating her feet should help the vertigo, probably caused by a sudden drop in blood pressure. It wasn't uncommon for blood pressure to fluctuate during pregnancy.

Cole knelt beside her.

"Don't look at me like that," she snapped.

"How am I looking at you? Like I'm worried you're going to pass out?"

"I'm not, so stop placating me."

"Let me take your blood pressure."

"Don't you dare. I'm fine. That kid just caught me by surprise was all. Call his father. Do it now."

Cole shook his head, giving her a look of exasperation. He stood and pulled the department phone from his scrub pocket. "Do you want to give me the number, or do I have to look it up on the patient's record?"

"Call the unit clerk. Get her to connect you."

Cole did as Tamara had bidden him. "Hello, is this Mr. Pack? I'm Cole Edwards, a nurse in the emergency department at Arms Forks. Your son Devon has been admitted as a patient here, and you need to come as soon as you can so that we can treat him....I'm sorry. I can't.... I understand that, but the hospital policy is that I cannot give you any information on the patient other than to tell you he is a patient here, and we need you to come here so that you can give written consent." Cole sat on a chair near Tamara. He turned, his eyebrows shooting up to his hairline. "Dr. Wallace?" His eyes dropped to hers, and she shook her head vehemently. "She's not available." A grin lit Cole's face. "Excuse me, but it isn't standard practice for the parents of patients to consult with one of the ER doctors just because he demands it.... I'm sure you are.... I'm sure you will." His eyes widened. "Placating you? I apologize. Very good. Goodbye."

He pressed the end button and looked at her. "What? Is placate the word of the day, and no one told me?"

From her pocket, Tamara's own cell phone rang. Cole's snickered. "Wonder who that could be."

Tamara retrieved the phone and looked at the screen. Sure enough, it was Nick. She hit the icon so the call would go straight to voice mail. In less than a minute, he texted her.

Call me ASAP.

Tamara snorted. As if.

She sat up. "We need to get back to work."

"How do you feel?"

"Wonderful."

Cole snickered and held out his hand to help her to her feet.

Another text from Nick.

I'm sorry I didn't tell you about Devon. I know you're angry. Please call me so I know if he's okay.

When Tamara glanced at Cole, she noted he was looking at the screen on her phone as well.

"You're the attending. The attending can disclose information to family over the phone."

"I don't want to talk to him right now. He has a son, and he never told me."

"Who is he to you?" Cole's eyes shot to her stomach for a second. He was wondering if Nick was the baby's father.

"It's complicated."

"It always is."

"He's Miranda's grandfather."

"Oh. So, he's not....?"

"I told you, it's complicated."

"Okay. It's complicated. He's obviously worried about Devon. He's driving from Charleston to get here. Do you really want him driving when he's distracted because he doesn't know if his son is living or dead?"

They walked toward the nurses' station, and the unit clerk spotted Tamara. "Dr. Wallace, you have a phone call on line one. Nicolaus Pack."

Tamara strode over to the physician's desk and picked up the phone. Keep it professional, she counseled herself. You've talked to many frantic parents of patients. This is no different.

Except you made love to this parent three nights ago.

Tamara shut the thought out of her mind.

"Dr. Wallace," she barked.

"Tamara—"

"Devon appears to have a fractured radius. He is in pain, but he appears to be okay other than that. The hospital needs your written consent before we can treat him."

"I know I should have—"

"I am ending this call now. Goodbye." Tamara placed the phone back in its cradle.

The jerk.

She had a patient with abdominal pain she needed to assess and a follow up to diagnose once she looked at the labs. She didn't have time for complicated situations like the one in room 14. Tamara picked up the phone and called Dr. Edisco, the best orthopedist in town. He wasn't on call, but he owed Tamara a favor, and she didn't want just anyone working on Devon.

Cole set a paper on the desk in front of her. "We just received a fax giving written permission to treat Devon Pack."

Tamar picked up the paper and read it. It was a general consent form, not hospital issued, but good enough for them to go forward. "Does this mean he's not coming?"

"Oh, he's coming." Cole handed her another paper. "This is the cover letter."

Devon Pack's father, Nicolaus Pack, is en route and is available by cell phone for consultation. The note was signed by...Aha....Jessica Adams, Nick's secretary, the same one who couldn't remember the proper pronunciation of Tamara's name.

Tamara logged on to her computer, opened the treatment program, and ordered an X-ray. Maybe by the time Nick got here, they could have the results back, Dr. Edisco would be here to set the arm, and Tamara could... what? What was she going to say to him?

"Okay. Order is in. Go ahead and call radiology. I'd like this to go as quickly as possible."

"Afraid Daddy Pack might loiter too long?"

"Don't call him that," Tamara threw over her shoulder as she strode toward the patient in 3 with abdominal discomfort.

In forty minutes, Jerry, who manned the front desk in the lobby, accompanied Nick down the corridor. Tamara watched them go by as she stood next to a patient lying on a gurney in the hallway. Nick didn't see her as she studied him, his eyes like flint, and his jaw tight, his lips pressed in a thin line. Jerry indicated Nick should go in the room, and some interior warning propelled Tamara to excuse herself and go into room 14.

Nick's voice reached her before she entered the room. "What are you even doing here in Arms Fork anyway? I've been calling your cell phone for hours. I've told you and told you I don't care what you're doing, when I call, you pick up."

Tamara slid the door shut, and reached up to close the curtain. Turning around, she noticed Nick standing in a combative posture and Devon still cradling his arm with shoulders hunched and head bowed.

Anger simmered in Tamara's gut. She crossed her arms over her chest. "His phone was dead. Otherwise, I'm sure he would have answered."

"Is that the excuse he gave you?"

"Yes, and I believe him. So let's focus on Devon's treatment right now."

"You shouldn't even be treating him!" Nick faced Devon. "What were you doing here?"

Tamara marched toward Nick and stood between him and his son. "Nick." She crooked her head toward the door. "Would you come with me please?"

"No. I want to know what the hell he's doing in Arms Fork, Kentucky."

She reached up and pinched his sleeve, nudging him toward the corner of the room. She walked a few steps around so that his back was to Devon, and he was, in effect, blocking Devon's view of her. "There will be opportunity for you to have those questions answered." She squeezed his arm. "Later. Take a deep breath and focus on what he needs from you right now. He's been in pain for hours. He needs your love and concern, not for you to come in here and berate him."

"He's my son, and you're not going to tell me…"

"He may be your son, but he's my patient." Tamara spoke in low tones, hoping Devon wasn't able to hear her. "I have written consent from you to treat him. In the best interest of my patient, you will calm down right now, or I'll have security escort you out to the lobby. Do you understand?"

"You can't do that. He's a minor, and I'm his father," Nick snapped, and snatched his sleeve out of her grasp.

"If you are impeding care of my patient, yes, I can." Tamara went over to the phone. She picked up the receiver watching Nick all the while. She dialed the four digit extension. "Hello, this is Dr. Wallace. I need a security escort from E.D. Room 14. Thank you."

Devon's gaze ricocheted from Nick to Tamara and back. "Whoa," he breathed.

Nick narrowed his eyes. "I do not appreciate you using your position to get back at me for…."

Tamara made a shushing sound. "This is me taking care of my patient. I understand that you were worried about Devon but jumping all over him isn't the way to show it."

"You have no idea—none—what it's…."

Gil, the security guard entered the room. He looked at Tamara, and she nodded toward Nick. "Can you escort Mr. Pack to the family quiet room and wait with him there until I arrive?"

"Yes, ma'am."

"Thank you."

Without a word, Nick walked out with Gil.

"I can't believe you kicked my dad out," Devon said. "You're a badass. Dr. Badass."

Tamara laughed. "It's just until he calms down a little. He was genuinely worried about you."

The little smile on Devon's face disappeared. "No, he wasn't. He just likes to control my every move. Me being here, meeting you, that wasn't in his plan, so he hates that it happened," he said quietly.

"I would venture to say nothing about me has been in your father's plan. But that's something we all will talk about after you get your arm set and casted and after your dad pulls himself together. In the meantime, I'm going to send Cole in here with a shot for pain. I want you to take it."

"No. I told him already, I don't need any pain meds. I was joking before about it, but I do not want it."

"Why not?"

"Because I don't. It doesn't even hurt that much anymore."

"It still hurts, I think, and it's going to really hurt when the doctor does the reduction."

"I thought you were my doctor."

"I'm the E.D. doctor. For bone fractures, I defer to a specialist. Dr. Edisco, the orthopedist, will set your arm. It's a brief procedure, but can be painful."

Devon's jaw tightened in an expression Tamara had seen in his father. "I can take it."

She looked at him steadily. "But you don't have to."

Dr. Edisco arrived, looked at the X-rays, and began an exam of Devon. Tamara used the opportunity to go to the quiet room, a space dedicated to people who had a family member as a patient in the emergency department. It was often used for medical consults with those families or a waiting place when the patient was being attended by medical staff. Nick sat on one of the couches, his elbows resting on his knees. He looked up as she walked in and shut the door. The tension and anxiety on his face disappeared, and in its place anger.

She reached up, took off her stethoscope, and placed it on the low table. Then she sat down next to him. He watched her.

"I want to set aside being a doctor for a few minutes,"

she said. "I want to be the woman who made love to you the other night."

Nick straightened and moved against the back of the couch, but he never broke his gaze with her.

"I was very angry that you haven't told me about Devon. Why haven't you?"

"I didn't bring it up initially because I didn't trust you, and then I couldn't figure out how to bring it up because it seemed like I should have already told you by now."

Tamara nodded. "That explanation seems plausible. Now I'm angry because you've been neglecting him, and you haven't told him what's going on. Now, I know it's none of my business, but don't you think he deserves to know why you're spending so much time here?"

Nick sighed. He leaned forward again and laid his head in his hands. "He's a hard kid to talk to. I hardly know him. He was only two when Brenda left me."

"Then you're long overdue. Don't you think?" Tamara moved closer to him. She put her hand around his shoulders. "He's lost so much. He needs you. But however you want to handle this, I will follow your lead."

Nick raised his head and turned to her.

"Do you want him to know about Miranda?"

"Why is he even here? Does he already know about Miranda? About you?"

"I think he thinks you and I are involved. He's brought it up, but each time I redirected him. He didn't mention Miranda, so I don't know if he knows about her or not."

"How did he find out? How did he know you worked here?"

Tamara shrugged. "Maybe he became curious when you were gone in the evenings. Maybe he followed you."

Nick turned toward the far wall, realization blanketed his face. "Oh, shit."

"What?"

"One of the times when Miranda called me—one morning—Devon came in right after I got off the phone. He must have overheard me talking to her."

"That was when she used my phone. He must have looked at your phone and gotten my name from your contacts. But how did he know I worked here?"

"Maybe he did an Internet search."

Tamara smiled. "We have smart children, don't we? I still can't believe Miranda was savvy enough to be able to steal my phone and call you. So, how do you want to handle it?"

"What else can we do? We tell him the truth."

"There's one more thing you probably should know. I called in Dr. Edisco. He's the best orthopedist in the tri-state. He and I have consulted about Devon, and we don't think he broke his arm skateboarding. He has no contusions, no other injuries we usually see in that kind of incident."

"What are you saying?"

"It's possible that it was self-inflicted. With a blunt object of some kind."

Nick's eyes widened.

Tamara continued. "He's left-handed, and the fracture is to his right arm, and with it being the radius." She held her arm out and demonstrated striking her forearm with her other hand. "I'm not saying he definitely tried to hurt himself. I'm just saying it's possible because what he told me doesn't match up to the injury. He also came in yesterday complaining of chest pain."

"What?"

"He requested me as a doctor, and when they told him I wasn't working, he disappeared."

Nick blew out a breath.

"So, if he faked the chest pain yesterday, and didn't get anywhere, found out today that I was here, well, a fracture would definitely require that he'd make it into the E.D. instead of just immediate care, which is for less serious cases."

Her hospital phone rang. She pressed the answer button and held it to her ear. "Dr. Wallace."

"It's Dr. Edisco. Are you with the patient's father?"

"Yes. We'll be right there." Tamara disconnected the call. She stood up. "Let's go consult with the orthopedist."

"What the hell am I supposed to do? My God, he intentionally broke his own arm?" The agony on Nick's face pulled at Tamara.

She picked up her stethoscope and walked toward the door, gesturing for him to follow her. "That's supposition. Just set aside that piece of knowledge for now. I think he was just desperate to find out who I was. With that in mind, please be very patient with him, but tell him he needs to take something for pain. Thus far, he's refused anything." Tamara opened the door, and they walked through it. "Do you know why?"

They arrived at the doors leading to the inner sanctum of the department. Tamara swiped her badge to allow them access.

"Because both his mother and brother had addiction problems. We've had conversations about whether he might be prone to addiction too."

They approached Devon's room. "An NSAID is better than nothing. It's not a narcotic, so it isn't...."

A nurse called out, "Dr. Wallace, room 4 STAT."

She shot an apologetic look to Nick. "I'm sorry. I'll come back as soon as I can."

Chapter Thirteen

Nick sat on the chair and watched Tamara, Dr. Edisco, and the nurse whose nametag identified him as Cole, set Devon's arm then place an air cast on it. If Nick hadn't been attracted to Tamara before, watching her efficiency and brilliance in her work environment would have changed his mind. Plus, she seemed to really like his kid. She kept coming in the room and typing on the laptop in the corner, and after two different nurses entered and summoned her elsewhere, Nick realized she had relocated her workstation to Devon's room.

She left once again when her pager sounded leaving the other doctor and Cole to finish.

Dr. Edisco took one more thorough survey of Devon's casted arm. "I want to see you in two days. The swelling will be down by then, and we'll put a plaster cast on." He peered at the teenager over his glasses. "You want to tell me how you really broke your arm?"

"Skateboarding."

"Uh-huh. Sticking to your story, huh? Well, all right then. Maybe Dr. B.A. can get it out of you."

Nick had only seen Tamara and Dr. Edisco. Damn, how many doctors did it take to fix an arm? "Who's Dr. B.A?"

The man turned to him and grinned.

"Your son has nicknamed Dr. Wallace. Dr. Tamara Badass."

Cole laughed.

The smile on the doctor's face faded. "Devon, the skateboarding." He shook his head. "Or however this happened, let this be the last time. You were lucky. But you must not push the luck, eh?"

Devon nodded slowly.

The doctor and Cole left a few minutes later. The silence in the room stifled Nick. He wondered when they could leave. Devon lay back on the bed with his arm resting on his chest, and his good arm pillowing his head as he watched the television mounted on the wall.

Tamara breezed in and went to the computer. She sat down and swiveled her stool to face him. "Well, Devon. Other than getting your paperwork ready for discharge, your care here is finished. You wanted this meeting with me, and now your father is here, what would you like to talk about?"

Devon's attention went from Tamara to Nick to Tamara again. Then back to Nick, as if Devon were watching a tennis match.

"If you wanted to know what was going on, why didn't you just...." Nick began.

"Ah, ah, ah, ah, ah," Tamara quieted Nick with the verbal sound and a harsh look. She turned back to Devon, with a relaxed smile. "Go ahead, Devon. Tell us what's on your mind."

The teen speared Nick with an angry gaze. "I wish you had told me that you had a girlfriend and a kid without me having to ask. I mean." He shook his head in disgust. "Geez, Dad."

What the hell? "A kid?" Nick thundered. "What are you talking about?"

He swung his attention to Tamara whose mouth hung open in shock.

Devon continued. "I heard you talking to her on the phone one morning. When were you going to tell me I have a sister?"

"A sister? You mean Miranda? She's not your sister. She's your...." Nick paused and wiped his hand over his face. "Reginald, before he died, he...." Nick blew out a breath. How could he explain this craziness?

"Your brother made a donation which made it possible

for me to have a child."

Devon's eyes narrowed. "Like money, right?"

"No. Not money. Sperm." Tamara spoke in her doctor tone.

Devon studied Tamara, and she stared back until her chin lifted.

"I never met him," she said carefully. "He made the donation at a fertility clinic, and I chose a candidate with genetic traits I liked. That candidate happened to be your brother Reginald. I was implanted with his donated sperm."

Devon blinked a few times. "Did you pay him?"

"I did not pay him, no. He was compensated by the fertility clinic for his donation, however."

Devon's expression lightened until a chuckle rose from his lips. "No way. No freakin' way." He lay back on the bed and chortled. "If the guys at school ever find out people will pay for them to jack off, that clinic's going to be overrun."

Irritation blanketed Nick's mind. "Devon," he snapped.

Tamara shook her head, a little smile lifted her lips.

What? She thought this was funny?

Devon continued to laugh. "What do they do? Put a guy in a room with a porno and a cup?"

"Actually, yes," Tamara said.

Devon's laughter stopped suddenly. "Really? Wow. How many donations can a...."

"Devon, that's enough."

Tamara smiled. "You have to be over eighteen anyway."

"And one sperm donor in the family is plenty," Nick said.

Nick noticed Tamara's smile disappeared. She cleared her throat. "Do you have any questions about my daughter Miranda?"

Devon rolled onto his side then sat up. "How old is she?"

"She's four."

"Weird."

"Would you like to see a picture of her?" Without

waiting for an answer, Tamara pulled out her phone and touched the screen. She appeared to be scrolling through some pictures as she walked to the bed. "Here she is at her birthday party when she turned four. Here she is holding our cat, Gary."

"Gary doesn't look happy."

"He doesn't like to play dress up, obviously. This is Miranda with my mother whom she calls Meemee. Oh. This day we went to the park, and she was feeding the ducks."

Devon smiled. Tamara showed him another picture, and his face fell.

"This is in the hospital the day Miranda got her PICC line in. She has leukemia, and she's taking chemotherapy. She calls her PICC line, her straw."

"Geez. That's…that's…." Devon shook his head.

"Life-threatening, yes. But I'm hopeful she will go in remission. The reason I contacted your father was because I needed some information from him about Miranda's treatment. Since Reginald had died, your father would still know his health history, and it might help Miranda get better." Tamara watched Nick as she spoke. Did she not want Devon to know Nick had been tested to be a bone marrow donor? Or was it that she didn't want him to know they'd hooked up in Atlanta?

"I can't believe it. She's so little to have cancer."

"She's tough." Tamara put her phone back in her pocket. "So, now you know. Was it worth breaking your arm for?"

"Yes."

"Next time, just ask your father. Or ask me. No more crazy stunts, okay?" She held out her hand to him.

He looked at her for a second before accepting the handshake. "You're a badass."

"You flatter me. Are you hungry?"

"Starving."

"I can order you a tray, but it may take a while. I bet your dad would get you something from McDonalds. It's just across the street. What do you like? A couple of Big Macs?"

Nick's own stomach growled. He realized he hadn't eaten since the eleven o'clock lunch meeting he'd had. He doubted Devon had eaten supper yet. Guilt nagged at Nick. It was after ten at night. Why hadn't it occurred to him that his son would be hungry?

"Of course, I'll go. Just tell me what you want, son," Nick said.

"Everything on the menu."

Nick had picked up enough food for all three of them, but Tamara was gone when he came back. She strode in one last time, accepted a hamburger, immediately opening the wrapper and biting into it.

"Thank you," she said between bites.

It occurred to him to make a comment about taking better care of herself, taking her dinner break when she was hungry, and to hell if the patients had to wait a little longer, but he doubted she'd appreciate his advice even if it was well-meant.

He handed her a bottle of water. "I wasn't sure what you liked to drink." Other than the wine they had shared in the hotel room and the water everyone had drank with dinner at her house, Nick didn't know her preferences.

"Water's good. I'm sorry I can't stay. The ER is filling up. Devon has his paperwork, so you all can leave. He shouldn't drive for twenty-four hours." She cast him an apologetic look. "If you want to leave your car or his car here, we can have security tag it for long term parking, and you can get it Saturday when you come over."

"Come over?" Devon asked.

"Yes. Your dad and I thought it would be nice for you two to visit my house and meet Miranda unless you have other plans?" She didn't even glance Nick's way, acting as if this visit was already set.

"I guess so."

"You don't have to meet her if you don't want to. She doesn't know about you yet, so it's your choice." Her easy-going manner demonstrated she wouldn't judge Devon whatever he decided.

"I want to meet her," he said firmly.

She did look up at Nick then, a question in her gaze. "You could come over for lunch."

"Eleven o'clock?" Nick asked. He wanted to lean down and kiss her, but Devon was watching them. Did he suspect their relationship was more than a connection with Miranda?

Hell, he himself didn't even know what they were to each other, except he couldn't quit thinking about her.

Nick drove them home. The hum of wheels against the road was the only sound in the car. He thought Devon had fallen asleep, until he spoke.

"Dad?"

"What?"

"How come you didn't tell me?"

Nick sighed. "I don't know." It wasn't that Nick had purposely withheld it from Devon. He'd just become so focused on Tamara and her daughter so quickly. It was just easier not to tell Devon anything. "Miranda is like a miniature version of Reg. All attitude, like he was when he was four. And it's been a lot to take in. Especially if she doesn't beat the cancer, I didn't want to say, hey, you've got a niece, then you having to deal with losing one more person. Know what I mean?"

"So, she's pretty bad off."

"Tamara says the leukemia is aggressive. She contacted me because she wanted me to be tested as a match for a bone marrow or blood cell transplant. It's the best bet for curing Miranda, but I wasn't a match. Still. Tamara says Miranda has a good chance with just the chemo."

"I like Tamara. She treats me like she cares what I think."

Nick inhaled guilt as if it were blowing from the dashboard vents.

"Dev. It was wrong of me not to tell you what was going on. I'm sorry."

"When I overheard you talking to Miranda, I thought I

finally understood."

"Understood what?"

"Why you resent me being here. Why you wish I had died in the car wreck too."

Denial rose immediately at Devon's words. Did he really believe that? Instead of reacting to the absurd comment, Nick decided to explore what was behind it. "Why would you think that?"

"Because you never wanted me and Reg, and after he and Mom died, and I came to live with you, you didn't act happy about it."

Nick had never badmouthed his wife in front of his son. He'd never criticized her, even when he talked about her alcoholism. He spoke about her addiction as a sickness because that's what he believed it was. Any resentment he had was against a system that had placed two kids with a woman because she was their mother, not because she was necessarily a good parent.

"I fought for custody for both of you, but I lost."

"That's not what Mom said."

"I can't help what she said, but I can show you the court papers if you like." Nick let that sink in for a moment. "I would never have wished your mother dead, but if there was anything good that came from that wreck, it's that you survived and I have you with me. I've never resented you, and I've failed as a parent if I came across that way. I've been distant lately. I realize that now. Finding out Reg had a kid, it's brought back all of the shit that he pulled before he died." Nick felt anger rising in him as he spoke. "It was just like him to pull some kind of stunt like this, and for what? Because he needed money?"

His last harsh question hung in the dark interior of the car, making Nick regret losing his control.

"Tamara seems happy to have Miranda. Something about Reg made her choose him as the sperm donor, and you have to admit, it's kind of cool that he has a kid. Like finding a Christmas present you forgot you hid six months later."

Nick's throat closed up at the insight of his son. He reached over and squeezed his shoulder. When he could speak again, he said. "I love you, son."

"Dad, I swear, you're such a softie. I bet you cried when you found out about Miranda."

Nick smiled. "I didn't cry until I found out Miranda knew the song I used to sing to Reg when he was little."

"What song?"

"It was the goodnight song. You probably don't remember me singing it to you. You were so young when your mom and I divorced."

Devon didn't respond.

"How's your arm?"

"It's okay." Devon turned his face toward Nick, a little smile on his face.

"What?"

"Did Badass see you cry like a baby?"

"As a matter of fact, she did." Warmth spread through Nick's chest when he remembered that night, "and she liked it."

****

Tamara arrived home about half past midnight. She went downstairs to Sandy's suite and found the woman watching television in the small sitting room. She looked up when her daughter walked in.

"Well, my goodness." Sandy glanced at the clock on the wall. "Is it that late? This movie is longer than I thought."

"I saw your light on and wondered if everything was okay."

Sandy muted the television. "Everything is fine. Miranda had a good night."

"Can I talk to you about something?"

She gestured Tamara to sit. "Of course. Is the baby okay?"

Tamara caressed her stomach. She hadn't felt even so much as a flutter. "As far as I know. I have another appointment in two weeks."

"I'd like to go. Do you think it's too soon for an ultrasound?"

"No. Not too early. We'll be able to hear the heartbeat."

"It'll be so wonderful having another baby in the house."

"Yes. I just hope Miranda won't be too upset by it. She's been the center of our world for her whole life."

"She'll love the new baby. You'll see." Sandy reached over and patted Tamara's stomach. "You sneaky thing. I don't know why you didn't tell me you were thinking about all of this. How was work?"

Tamara reached her fingers under her glasses and rubbed her eyes. "Illuminating. Nick has a son—another son—that I didn't know about."

"You saw Nick? He told you tonight?"

"No. His son, Devon, told me."

"He has a son? How old?"

"Sixteen. He overheard Nick talking to Miranda on the telephone. He thought Nick had another family he didn't tell Devon about. So, anyway, long story short, I invited Nick and Devon over Saturday for lunch."

Sandy's studied her daughter for a moment. "Really?"

"Yes. Really."

"It's certainly okay with me. I like Nick a lot, but what has changed your mind here? I thought you wanted to discourage Nick from getting close to Miranda."

"I think it's too late. Nick doesn't want to upset her by staying away from her when she wants to see him. Until she goes into remission, he and I decided we'd let her see him if she wants. But…." Tamara blew out a breath. "Devon might be a game changer for me."

"What do you mean?"

"He's a neat kid, Mom, but I saw it really bothered him that Nick didn't tell him about us. He was two when Nick and his mom divorced, and he barely knew Nick until he came to live with him after his mom and Reg were killed in the car wreck. I don't understand why Nick cares so much about Miranda and at the same time would neglect his own son who has already lost so much."

"What are you saying? You don't want Nick here anymore? Then why did you invite them over Saturday?"

"I want to help Devon. If Nick is so determined to be a part of Miranda's life, then I want Devon to be a part of her life too. I think Devon and Miranda could be really good for each other."

"He's sixteen, Tamara. Don't expect too much of him." Tamara heard the caution in Sandy's voice.

"I'm not expecting him to be anything other than a sixteen year old, but his dad, I expect a lot more. He can be a better father to his son, and I think it's time someone showed him that."

"I don't see that it's your business."

"He wants input on my kid. I can certainly return the favor."

"Nick is Miranda's grandfather, whereas you're not related to his child. It's not like you to hold a grudge or to be spiteful."

"This is about helping Devon. Nick is the only family he has, and you should have seen them tonight. First Nick berated him then he acted as if he was a stranger. Maybe if Devon is part of what Nick is building with Miranda, then he and Devon can get closer too."

Sandy shrugged. "I hope this doesn't backfire. If Nick truly is neglecting his son, then bringing him here so he can see his father with another child is likely going to make Devon jealous."

Tamara sat back. She hadn't thought of that. "I'll just have to be sure that doesn't happen."

"I'll try to help too. How sad to have lost your mother and brother then to have to live with a father you barely know."

****

Tamara slept late Saturday morning because she'd had to work a double when the midnight physician called in with the flu. She'd almost called Nick to cancel, but Sandy had let it slip that Nick was coming over with a surprise.

Tamara awoke after only an hour of sleep with Miranda pouncing on the bed.

"Mama. Mommmmy, do you know what surprise Nicky is bringing me?"

Tamara opened bleary eyes and saw the everpresent SuperCooper hair. "What? Meemee said Nicky was bringing a surprise?"

"Yeah. What is it?"

"I think it's a person. Not a toy, so don't get too excited." Tamara yawned and turned on her side. Her hips had started to ache, an indicator that her body was adjusting to the new life inside. She closed her eyes.

"Hello. It's me."

Tamara's eyes flew open and saw Miranda holding her phone in front of her face.

"Hello, me," Nick's voice said through the phone.

Chapter Fourteen

"Wanna see Mommy? She's still asleep." Miranda scrambled down to lie next to her mom, holding the phone screen in front of both of them.

Eeep! When had Miranda figured out Face to Face chat?

"No fair," Tamara said at the blur in front of her. "I don't have on my glasses, so I can't see you."

"You're still asleep, and it's almost ten in the morning?"

Tamara reached and picked up her glasses from the chest of drawers. "I pulled a double last night. I haven't been home long." She settled back down next to Miranda and looked at Nick on the small screen. He was handsome, as always. She caught a glimpse of herself in the corner of the screen. "Oh, my gosh. I look like a hag."

"I like when your hair is all crazy, Mommy. It makes you look like a witch."

Tamara laughed. She turned her face to her daughter. "That makes you a witch daughter."

"I think I have a hat for that."

"You probably do, thanks to Nicky, who bought every hat in the mall."

"Should we reschedule?" Nick's voice brought Tamara's attention back to the phone.

"What's re-shed-ull?" Miranda asked.

"He's asking if they should not come today, and come another day instead."

"Noooo, Nicky! Noooo."

"There's your answer." Casually, Tamara reached up and attempted to smooth down her hair.

"I like your crazy hair. Don't try to tame it." Nick winked and smiled wickedly. "We could come later. I need to run a few errands anyway."

"What's errands?"

"It means I have some things to do, like buying casual clothes. Devon informed me khakis are too formal for a Saturday date."

Tamara's breath hitched at the word date. He didn't mean it like that. He meant a get together—kids and grandmas included.

"Can't you come over right now?" Miranda asked.

Tamara covered a yawn. "Just let us know when. We have food for a picnic up in Miranda's tree house."

"Are you bringing me a surprise? Meemee says you are."

"I guess I am then."

"Good. Hurry up, Nicky. I'll put my witch hair on to match Mommy's."

Tamara arose to shower before the visit hoping to look more presentable than the face Nick had seen in their phone chat. The doorbell chimed at noon.

Miranda still had on her SuperCooper cape, but had found red witch hair and a purple witch hat. The hideous ensemble somehow worked on the four year old who ran to the door and flung it open.

"Hi." The little girl's greeting reached Tamara in the kitchen cutting chicken salad sandwiches into triangles.

Sandy wiped her hands on a towel. "I'll go."

Tamara nodded and wrapped cellophane around the plate and placed it in the hamper. She surveyed the rest of the contents for the picnic. Yes, that was everything. She picked it up and carried it to where the voices sounded in the loft. Ascending the stairs, she heard Miranda say something and Devon respond.

On the landing, Tamara saw Miranda acting as hostess, retrieving canned drinks from the cooler they had left there earlier. Devon, Sandy, and Nick were already seated at the two card tables they had set up, but when Nick noticed her, he stood up. He cleared his throat and cast a glance at Devon who stood as well.

Tamara's breath caught when she saw Nick in blue jeans and a black T-shirt. She'd never seen him dressed so casually, and he sure wore the look well. She realized they were standing up because she had entered the room. The chivalrous gesture made her want to grab Nick and kiss him. Tamara smiled at the impetuous feeling. Hormones. It's probably the hormones.

"Mommy, this is my uncle." Miranda set a can of pop on the table in front of Devon. "Did you know I had an uncle?"

"Yes, I knew that." Tamara set the picnic hamper on the table and began to unpack it.

"His arm's broke," the little girl added.

"Broken," Miranda corrected.

Devon and Nick resumed their seats. Devon's air cast had been replaced with a fluorescent green plaster cast.

"Isn't his arm pretty?"

"Yes, it is," Tamara risked another glance at Nick. Her heart skipped a beat when she saw he watched her.

"I want a broken arm."

Tamara laid out the food on the table. "No."

"How come? Cause I've already got leukemia?"

"Yes, and you shouldn't be so greedy," Sandy said. "One malady in a body is enough."

Tamara shot her mother a dark stare. Good grief, the things that woman says.

"What's a malady?"

"It's when something's wrong, like being sick," Sandy said.

Tamara noticed Miranda had sandwiched herself between Nick and Devon. She looked up at her uncle. "Is your arm sick? Is that how comes it's broken?"

"Nah. I just did something stupid and broke it."

"Can I feel your arm sock?"

"It's called a cast," Tamara put the basket down on the floor and claimed the last available chair, thankfully across from Devon who had moved his arm in front of Miranda. She ran her hands across the cast, then rapped it with her knuckles.

By the time Tamara passed around the ice cream sandwiches for dessert, she found it hard to ignore the mutual connection between the children. She wasn't surprised Miranda was drawn to Devon, but the teenager acted as if he had always been a part of Miranda's life. And the little girl certainly enjoyed talking to him. Tamara would have never believed a sixteen year old boy could be so patient and kind to a small child.

Devon popped the last bite of the treat in his mouth and chewed. "So, when can I get tested to be a donor for the littlest witch here?"

"No," Nick said.

"You can't," Tamara said at the same time. She looked at him, and he returned her gaze.

"I know why I'm saying no. Why are you saying no?" Nick asked.

Tamara shook her head. "This is something we should discuss privately."

"I want to be part of the discussion since it's about me," Devon said.

"Yeah. I want to be part of the discussing too," Miranda added. "Since it's about us."

Devon grinned down at her. "You tell 'em, Little B.A."

Miranda's face lit as she gazed up at her uncle.

"Devon." Nick shot his son a look of disapproval at his son. "Don't call her that."

"What does that mean, Little B.A?" Sandy asked.

"I'll tell you later, Mom."

With the meal finished, Tamara suggested she, Nick, and Devon go to the hospital and retrieve Devon's car. On the way to the door, Nick suggested, "I'll drive."

Tamara held up her keys. "I should drive. I can get closer to the car from the physician's parking lot."

Nick acquiesced, and it felt like a victory of sorts so she pushed it a little more as they stood next to her SUV. "Let Devon ride in the front."

"Why?"

"Because I want to ask him about his arm."

"Ask me. I was at the appointment too."

Tamara arched an eyebrow at him.

He made a sound of disgust and moved around Devon to the back door. "Do you enjoy emasculating me in front of my son?" He grated.

"Somewhat."

Devon burst out laughing. Tamara's attention shifted back to Nick, and she noted the sardonic smile curve his lips. They entered the vehicle, and Tamara backed out of the garage.

"Tell me about your visit with Dr. Edisco."

"He put a cast on my arm."

"Obviously. What did he say?"

"I dunno. The usual stuff."

An angry sigh came from the back seat. He leaned forward. "Devon, she is attempting a conversation with you, although why she'd want to when you're acting like an ass I—"

Tamara placed her hand behind her in a halt gesture. Surprisingly, Nick sat back and stopped talking. "Devon, what were your discharge instructions?"

"Huh?"

"What kinds of things are you allowed or not allowed to do?"

"Oh. Don't get it wet. No sharp objects underneath, so I'll have to find another place for my shank."

Tamara let his quip pass without comment. "Did he say anything about skateboarding?"

Devon waited a few seconds before he answered. "No."

"That's because he doesn't think you broke your arm skateboarding," Tamara said.

"Look. I've already said what I did was stupid."

"Was this stupid thing you did with the help of someone else?"

Another pause, then, "I refuse to answer that question

on the grounds that it may incriminate someone else."

"You cannot invoke the fifth amendment on the grounds that it may incriminate a third party. It is a privilege you may only use for yourself," Nick said.

"I hope you know now you can call me or come to me if you want to talk."

"Or, here's an idea, why didn't you ask me instead of going behind my back and pulling such a damn fool stunt like breaking your own arm."

"Dad, I gave you lots of opportunities to tell me, and you never did. I even asked you where you were all night, and you just blew me off."

"I already explained—"

"Yes, you did. I get it." Devon spoke in a clipped tone, reminding Tamara of Nick when he'd been angry. "I hope you get it too, and can we be done with this?"

"Yes, Devon, we can," Tamara said.

They rode in silence for a few moments. "Since we can talk, why can't I be tested as a bone marrow donor for Miranda?"

"You're too young," Tamara said. "At sixteen, you haven't reached the age of consent to be able to donate."

"I can donate blood."

"Not without your father's permission. Not until you're seventeen," Tamara countered.

"That's four months away. What's four months' matter?"

"I appreciate that you want to do this. But there are reasons why these guidelines are in place. You're still growing, and if there was a complication, I wouldn't want your life compromised."

"It won't be. They probably do this all the time. I thought as a doctor, you would have more confidence in the people who would take the donation. You being in the medical profession, and all."

Tamara's resolve cracked a bit at the young man's argument. What if he was a match? And what if the donation had no glitches? What if it put Miranda in remission? Tamara glanced at Nick who glared out the window. Obviously, Devon, too, had inherited his father's stubbornness. It must be a dominant trait.

But the bending of her will was her maternal yearning for Miranda to be cured no matter the cost. It wasn't fair to Nick to put his son at risk even if it was small. And Devon couldn't understand that. At sixteen, he thought he was invincible.

"As a doctor, I know what is involved. Though the risk is minimal, I am not willing to take it at this point. You mean too much to your father. He's already lost one son. I will do what I have to to protect you, as will he. This is why I don't think it's a good idea."

"It's just a procedure. They don't even call it a surgery."

Tamara reached over and patted Devon's arm. "You are so sweet to want to help Miranda. But she is on the marrow recipient list. It's possible we will still find a donor."

"You're not going to find a donor because no one knows about the recipient list. I didn't know about it, and I'm on the web all the time." Devon wasn't ready to let this go yet.

"And how often do you search for organ and tissue donation sites when you're on the Internet?"

"Well, okay, I'll give you that. But I didn't know to look until now."

The hospital loomed in front of them. Tamara maneuvered the car into the designated parking area. "This is not for you to worry about. I appreciate that you want to be tested, but right now the answer is no."

Devon shook his head, and a nerve ticked in his young jaw.

Oh, you are your father's son.

Tamara depressed the brake behind a black Acura.

"Here we are," she said.

"How'd you know that was his car?" Nick asked from the backseat.

"Kanawha plate, a security parking permission hanging from the mirror, and the most popular skateboard logo prominently displayed on the bumper." She met his gaze in the mirror. "Am I wrong?"

"Badass." The smile she'd seen on Nick she now saw on his son's face as he nodded at her and exited the vehicle.

Nick opened the back door and claimed the vacated spot. Tamara inhaled deeply without realizing it, and she caught Nick's musky cologne. She resisted the urge to lean over and bury her face in his neck for another whiff.

Nick rolled down the window. "Meet us back at Tamara's," he called to his son.

Tamara moved her car forward and waited until Devon started the engine and backed out of the parking space then she drove to her house. Nick didn't speak, and Tamara wondered if he were angry with her. Ten minutes into the trip, she broke the silence.

"I'm sorry if I monopolized the conversation about Devon donating. I just feel very strongly about this."

"I don't feel right about it. My gut clenches just thinking about him undergoing a procedure. But I'm being a selfish prick not to want him to donate."

"He's your son. Your only son. Of course you want to protect him at all costs."

"Yes, but he could save Miranda's life."

All of the nerve-endings stood at attention at the truth he verbalized. It took everything in Tamara not to latch onto it.

"That's too much to put on a sixteen-year-old. Don't make him responsible for saving her."

"She's your child. How can you say no? Argue with me. Tell me I need to give him permission to be tested."

Miranda took a steadying breath. "I may have an alternative."

"What?"

"I could have a baby compatible with Miranda's genetic blood type. The cord blood would be enough to infuse in her. That way no one has to undergo any procedure." Tamara couldn't look at him as she spoke.

"I thought you said you couldn't have any more kids."

"No. What I said was birth control wasn't an issue for me."

She could almost hear him working it out in his head and she dreaded what was coming. *Please don't ask me if the baby is yours.*

He dug the heels of his hands in his eyes. "Because you're already pregnant."

Here it was. Finally. The truth. Out.

"Yes."

"Oh, dammit. Oh, dammit."

Words poured through her mind about reassuring him she didn't expect him to take any responsibility. That it had been her decision. That he owed her nothing.

"Is it Reginald's?"

"What?"

"When you went to the sperm bank, were you able to get Reginald's sperm?"

Oh. He thought.... Relief and unease washed over her. "No."

"But you found a donor that was close."

"Yes. I had been wanting another baby anyway. If the baby's a match, then Miranda will get the cord blood, and the chances of remission are over 90 percent."

"When will you know?"

"I'll have amniocentesis in a few months, and I'll know then."

"You did this because I was too much of a sonofabitch to be tested. You had to go to the damn sperm bank and get implanted with someone else's sperm. That's what you meant about doing anything, wasn't it?"

"It doesn't matter, Nick. You couldn't give her the marrow anyway. It's a moot point, and I wanted another baby. If it's a match, it will be a win/win for everyone. Especially me."

"What about us?"

Tamara chose her words carefully. "You are Miranda's grandfather. Our plan was that once she is in remission, you will ease out of her life. I see no reason to deviate from that plan. You have no obligation to me. You certainly don't have any obligation to my baby."

"That's all I am to you—Miranda's grandfather?"

Tamara didn't answer. She didn't know how. No, he was more than that. She was in love with him. But she'd seen how her own father had broken her mother's heart. Tamara would not entangle a man because he'd impregnated her.

"I don't know what you are to me. I just know I'm scared, Nick, because I like you. I really like you, but I'm not good at this. I've never been involved with someone other than that debacle in college, and the timing could have been better for all of us."

"You sure as hell can say that again."

"I understand if you don't want to get intimate with me again. I don't blame you. You didn't know I was pregnant. It's probably a turnoff." Tamara shrugged, hoping he would believe this lie, one more in all of the lies of misleading and misdirection she'd told in ten short minutes.

When they arrived at the house, she left the garage door open, so he could walk to his car. "I'm kind of tired. I'm going to go in and lie down. Miranda's probably down for her nap, too." She opened the car door and stood without waiting for him to respond. She walked toward the kitchen entrance.

"Tamara."

She turned and saw the tension all over his face. "I really like you too. That's hard for me to admit."

She nodded. "Me too."

"Can I call you later?"

"Sure." He was just being nice—trying to make a gracious exit. But Tamara saw the hunted look in his eyes. He wanted to get away. "I'll see you, Nick." She ascended the three stairs to the door and walked inside the house without looking back.

Chapter Fifteen

Tamara assigned Nick to a little room in her mind and locked him in there. Whenever his image or the sound of his voice escaped, she'd put them right back in and think of something else. Late one afternoon, Devon showed up at the hospital, along with a friend of his from school. Bonita, the unit clerk, led them back to the staff breakroom.

"Hi." Tamara covered her surprise as Devon introduced her to Mitch Hughes, the young man with him. "What are you guys doing in Arms Forks?"

Mitch and Devon grinned. "Doing a little boarding. The parking deck here is killer."

"Skateboarding?"

Devon nodded.

"Skateboarding is prohibited in the parking deck, and you shouldn't be doing that with your arm."

"Dr. Edisco didn't say I couldn't."

"I'm saying you shouldn't."

Devon knocked his cast with his fist. "This thing is tougher than any skate pads. I don't see a problem."

"Does your dad know you're here? Trespassing on hospital property?"

Devon reached behind him and picked up a bag from the table. "It's not trespassing if I have legit business. I heard Dad bellyaching that you're too busy to go get supper when you're working, and how he worries about you, so here's you some food, Dr. Badass."

Tamara accepted the bag with a smile. She opened it and looked inside. Two wrapped burgers and a large order of fries. Her stomach growled in anticipation.

She picked up the package of fries and began to eat.

"When did your dad bellyache about me? The night you were in the ER, I bet," she said between bites.

"No. Yesterday, he was in a pissy mood. Yelling at me for nothing, so I said something about you and Miranda to distract him, then he went on a rant about you. 'How is she going to take care of a kid when she doesn't even take care of herself?'so I figured I come over and help out, then the next time he rides my butt, I'd have some leverage."

"Leverage, huh?" Tamara's stomach fluttered, but not from hunger this time. And not the baby. That flutter was an oh-boy-he's-worried-about me. "This is not a payoff for my silence. If he asks me, I'm going to tell him everything."

Not that he would ask her. She hadn't heard from him since the day he'd found out she was pregnant. Still. He was worried enough about her that he'd told Devon.

That was something, wasn't it?

When she arrived home from work at half past midnight on Friday, Nick's car was in her driveway, and—oh—he was inside. By the time she parked in the garage, he stood next to his car wearing blue jeans and an unzipped jacket over a golf shirt.

"Hey," she said shouldering her bag. "Did you spend the evening with Miranda?"

"No." He crossed his arms over his chest. "I just got here a few minutes ago."

"Oh." She couldn't read his expression in the dark. Why was he here? Had he found out Devon had come over to the hospital? "Want to come inside?"

"Yes." He began to walk toward her.

Nervousness revved up her heart. She placed her hand on her chest and breathed deeply. Adopting calm she didn't feel, she led him into the house, closing the garage door on the way. In the kitchen, she moved toward the back stairs. "I need to get a shower. If you want to go in the living room, I'll be back down in about fifteen minutes."

His emerald gaze dropped, and then met hers again. "Is it okay if I check on Miranda?"

Intensity blossomed in her chest at his question. How was she not supposed to fall in love with him when he obviously cared so much about her daughter?

Going upstairs, she shed her clothes and showered, quickly washing her hair and body knowing Nick was waiting on her. What if she put on the black pajamas? Was that pathetic? She turned off the shower, and opened the stall door. Pulling a towel from the rack, she stepped out of the cubicle and began to dry her body.

"Tamara." Nick's voice stopped her.

Tamara picked up her glasses from the shelf next to the shower. Nick sat on the foot of her bed with his hands clasped between his knees watching her. Tamara wrapped the towel around her body to cover herself.

"I didn't want to startle you, so I thought I better let you know I was here."

Embarrassment and anticipation battled for control of her emotions. She walked to the sink and out of his sight. Picking up her brush, she started the arduous task of combing through her hair. "What do you want?"

He appeared in the doorframe, and their eyes met in the mirror. She clutched the towel to her.

"You," he said. "Are you too tired to want me back?"

She shook her head.

He approached her, never breaking eye contact. "Miranda is asleep. It hurts to see her without the wig." He gestured for the brush, and Tamara surrendered it. He ran the bristles through her locks. When the brush encountered a tangle, he pinched the hair and gently worked it free. "It's odd, too, like she's not Miranda. But some sick kid you see on a cancer hospital commercial."

Tamara watched him as he focused on grooming her. She wanted so much to kiss him, to ask him to make love to her, but she couldn't. She couldn't do any of those things. She could only stand there scared to death because of how much she wanted him.

At last, he finished his task by moving her hair to fall

over her left shoulder. Leaning into her, he placed the brush on the counter. His body spooned hers, and Tamara squeezed her eyes shut to block out the image of them together and the tingling at her thighs and breasts and every other part of her that wanted him even closer.

One of his hands settled on her stomach, the other gripped the counter and he nudged into her backside. Her eyes flew open and settled on the alluring image of her and Nick behind her, his verdant gaze drawing her in.

"I want to take a picture of us like this, so when I'm not with you, I can look at this image and remember how lovely you look and feel in front of me."

"Absolutely not."

He dropped his head and kissed her exposed shoulder. "Do you really need that towel?"

"With the light on in front of the mirror and you? Yes."

She watched his hand disappear in the front fold of the towel, mesmerized by the simultaneous vision and taction of him, of them together. "I want to see what a pregnant doctor looks like."

His fingers stroked her stomach before moving northward and palming a breast. His lips fastened on the corded skin where her neck and shoulder met, and he sucked. Tamara couldn't help it, she ground into him, but she kept a death grip on the towel.

"Let's go in the bedroom," she said unsteadily gripping his thigh with her other hand.

"Uh-huh." He nipped her shoulder, piercing her with a predatory gaze. "I like this venue." He caressed the peak of her breast until Tamara lost sense of anything but his fingers. She cried out in pleasure and finally turned around, the towel falling as she did so. She grabbed his shirt and pulled him to her, landing her mouth on his, needing him, needing him right now.

"Take off your shirt." She pushed up the material then tugged at the button on his pants. "Nick, take off your shirt now."

He did so, while she lowered his zipper. In seconds, his clothes lay on the floor. He grasped her hips and perched her on the counter, all the while kissing her. Tamara nestled his hips between her knees, loving the contact of bare skin to bare skin.

"I don't want to hurt you or the baby," he said breathlessly. "Are you sure we're okay to do this?" He crouched and rained kisses across her collarbone and lower.

"We've already done this," she reminded him then gasped when his mouth closed over her nipple. She locked her legs around him. "Oh, please, I want to do this again."

Nick straightened, bundled her rear into his hands and pushed into her. "Tell me," he said. "Tell me anytime if I'm hurting you, and I'll stop."

"Don't. Don't you ever stop."

Later, they lay intertwined on Tamara's bed. Nick had several locks of her hair in between his hands, corkscrewing the curls around his fingers.

"I want to apologize," he said suddenly. "I wish you had told me sooner you were pregnant, but I get it about doing whatever it took to cure Miranda, about a plan to have a baby, and I understand how awkward it was to tell me."

Tamara watched him play with her hair. She was afraid to say much, that she might say too much.

"I think...." He turned on his side to face her. "I think something pretty amazing is happening here." His hand cupped her hip. The intimate gesture—or maybe it was Nick's admission, made her lose her breath. "Tamara, I never thought I'd want to get involved, to love someone again, to be a family again, but this is feeling so good, so damn good. Even you having a baby, it all feels so right."

Her chest ached, and she realized she'd been holding her breath. There was no way he meant it. He wanted to be with her? Really?

His beautiful green eyes roved over her face. "Is any of this resonating with you?"

She couldn't speak, so she just nodded then closed the

distance between them, hugging him tightly.

Oh, please don't let this be a dream.

She touched her lips to his, and deepened the kiss immediately wanting to seal the truth of his confession, wanting to cement this moment for all time.

A whimper sounded from the baby monitor, then another one. Tamara drew back, and she and Nick stared at each other waiting and listening.

"I better go check on her." Tamara sat up and moved away from Nick on the bed. She opened her closet and withdrew her terry robe, putting it on as she left the room.

"Mommy," Miranda's whimper reached her even before she entered. The nightlight illuminated dark stains against Miranda's light colored gown and more on the sheet. A coppery aroma hung heavy in the air. Tamara hit the light switch, and saw blood. Blood everywhere.

"Oh, Miranda, honey."

"Mama. Mommy!" she screamed becoming fully awake.

Miranda wrenched the sheet away.

"Just calm down. Mommy's here. Mommy's right here."

Where? Where was the blood coming from? Tamara gripped Miranda's gown and ripped it apart, buttons flew through the air.

"No! No! Ahhh, not my SuperCooper gown. Mommy," she cried.

Blood steadily fell from the open wound where Miranda's PICC line should have been. Tamara palmed the cuff of her sleeve and pressed it against her daughter's chest to stop the flow of blood. Tamara pried open her daughter's blood drenched fist and saw the plastic tube.

"Oh, my heavens!" Sandy appeared in the room, and behind her Nick with no shirt, his jeans still unbuttoned.

"What happened?" Nick asked.

"She's pulled out her PICC line. We've got to get to the hospital."

"I'll call 911," Sandy said.

"No. We'll take her ourselves." Tamara unbelted her

robe and shrugged out of it. "Mom, hold this firmly against her. Nick, finish getting dressed." She strode from the room, completely naked. Calmly and quickly, she dressed, grabbing underwear and clean scrubs. She didn't bother with socks and shoved her feet in her hospital shoes because they were the first pair she saw.

In three minutes, they were on their way to the hospital. Tamara drove, and Nick sat in the backseat with Miranda keeping a towel against her. Tamara directed Sandy to put some things together in a suitcase in case Miranda would need to be admitted. And to meet them there as soon as she had the bag packed.

Tamara handed her phone to Nick and gave him the number of the emergency department then engaged the vehicle's blue tooth.

"Emergency Department."

"Rachel, it's Tamara Wallace."

"Oh, hey, Dr. Wallace."

"My daughter Miranda's PICC line has come out. She's bleeding from the site, and it's not clotting. We're on our way to the E.D. right now. Please call Fred Thomas, and tell him to get to the hospital STAT."

"Okay."

"I'm pulling up to the ambulance entrance in twelve minutes. Miranda's blood type is A positive. I want a unit of blood waiting when I get there. Also, call in the pediatric team, and be ready for us."

"Will do. Be careful."

Before Tamara had the SUV in park, Nick had the door open and carried Miranda through the automatic doors into the hospital. On shaky legs, she followed him in, and handed her keys to the security guard. Without a word, he went outside, presumably to move her car.

Already, people surrounded the gurney, and Tamara couldn't see her daughter. Nick stood next to the wall, blood covering his shirt. Miranda screamed, and something inside Tamara screamed back. But she tamped it down. Years of medical training had taught her not to react. To keep calm.

Miranda's where she needs to be. I trust these people to take care of her.

"No! Nooooo! Mommy! Moooooommy! Help me!"

Agonized, she looked at Nick. His red-rimmed eyes made his green irises stand out even more.

"I should have been in there with her. I should have checked on her."

Nick gripped her shoulders. "I checked on her. She was fine. She must have done it after."

"I should have been there. I could have prevented it."

"You would have been asleep. You wouldn't have known until she cried out. You were right there when you needed to be."

Miranda screamed. The sound tore at Tamara's heart.

Virginia, a nurse, looked over her shoulder. "Dr. Wallace."

Nick squeezed her arms and let go. Tamara approached the staff attending Miranda. Someone moved giving her an opening.

Tamara reached for her daughter.

"No, Dr. Wallace. Get on the gurney."

Tamara climbed on the bed, and they placed her daughter on her lap. Immediately, Miranda went limp.

Oh, God, please, don't take her.

A wave of relief swept over the team. Miranda hadn't passed out. She had simply relaxed, and they were able to attend her. Dr. Thomas, Miranda's oncologist arrived a few minutes later, and he and Shelley conferred about the treatment plan.

As expected, the hospital admitted Miranda, and within an hour she slept in the pediatric unit on the fifth floor, her hand holding tightly to Tamara's through the bed railing.

"You should go home," Tamara said to Nick who sat on the couch in the corner.

He nodded and stood.

"Are you okay to drive back?

"Yes." He stood next to Tamara looking down at her. She resisted leaning into his leg, needing the contact. "I'll come back tomorrow."

"You don't have to."

"I know I don't. I want to. Is that okay?"

"Yes, it's okay."

Nick glanced at Sandy, and Tamara followed his gaze. Sandy shrugged. "Go ahead and kiss. It's not going to bother me."

Nick bent down and placed a chaste kiss on her lips. Tamara's other hand went around his neck. "Thank you, Nick. You were so wonderful tonight."

"I love you. I'll see you tomorrow," he whispered in her ear.

Tamara's arm dropped. Nick straightened and walked out of the room closing the door softly behind him.

He loves me. He loves me. He loves me.

The haze surrounding Tamara lifted, and she realized her mother watched her.

"When are you going to tell him he's going to be a father?"

"He knows I'm pregnant."

"That's not what I asked you. When are you going to tell him the baby's his?" Sandy arched her eyebrow and waited.

"It's complicated."

"I know it's complicated. Because you hooked up with Nick, Miranda is going to be both sister and aunt to that baby."

"The baby is—"

"He deserves to know."

"Why? So he can resent me and the baby for the rest of his life? I'm not doing that to him, and I'm not doing it to my baby. If he decides to be part of our lives, it will be because he loves us, and not because he feels obligated to us."

"Nick is not your father."

"Mom, trust me to handle this the way I think is best." Tamara leaned her head down on the railing, fatigue overcoming her.

She wished Nick had stayed. He probably would have if she'd asked him to, but it was late, and he'd already done so much already.

He told me he loves me. He actually said it.

She smiled.

****

Dr. Thomas scheduled Miranda for surgery Monday morning to have another PICC line placed. As a precaution, he wanted her to stay in the hospital through the weekend.

On Saturday afternoon, Nick sat in the hospital's recliner with Miranda on his lap. She seemed content to suck her thumb cuddled next to him. Tamara paced the room as she talked on the telephone with Sandy who had gone home.

"They're going to give her another unit of blood in the morning because her platelets are still low.... No, I can't because of the baby." Tamara's gaze met his.

She was going to have a baby. Regret niggled at him. If things had been different, if he'd met her sooner, maybe they could have had a baby together, and she wouldn't have had to go to a bank to be impregnated by a stranger's sperm.

The baby could have been his.

The door opened, and a woman breezed in. Nick tensed because he recognized her immediately. It was that tramp from the conference in Atlanta. What was she doing here?

"Mom, I've got to go." Tamara ended the call.

"Chocolate!" Miranda held up her hands in a give-me-a-hug gesture.

"Hey, girlie." She smiled at the girl, bent down, and hugged her briefly. Only when she straightened, did she acknowledge him. "Hi, Nick."

"What are you doing here?"

The woman looked back at Tamara, and Nick followed her gaze. He saw guilt written all over Tamara's face.

"Nick, this is my friend Charlotte."

Oh, hell.

Anger rose, tasting like bile in his throat.

Charlotte put her hands on her hips, her mouth open in disbelief. "You didn't tell him about me?" Her attention swung to Nick. "That's how she knew you were in Atlanta."

"So, your stalking at the conference was on behalf of Tamara." Nick lowered the footrest and stood, careful not to jostle his granddaughter. Gently, he laid her on the bed and covered her with the blanket. He bent down and kissed her cheek. "I'll see you later, okay?"

Miranda nodded at him.

Nick straightened, glaring at the women in turn.

Charlotte turned to Tamara. "Does he know about...?" She gestured to the other woman's stomach.

"Yes, he knows I'm pregnant, and that's—"

Charlotte's shoulders sagged in relief. "Oh, good! Because I was really sweating you not telling him."

"Charlotte—" Tamara said.

Charlotte smiled at Nick. "I'm glad you're cool with all of this. I mean, if the baby is a—"

"Charlotte," Tamara barked. She shook her head at her friend.

What was going on here? Nick watched the exchange in confusion, and then in an instant, it all fell into place.

The baby is mine.

Tamara watched him, tension evident in her face. How could she not tell him? And....

Her words in the hotel room came back to him. "Birth control is no longer an issue for me." He'd thought at the time she'd had her tubes tied. Then later when she told him she was pregnant, he'd assumed she had been pregnant when he'd met her. But she'd drunk wine with him that night. Of course, she wouldn't drink if she were already pregnant.

"Were you ever going to tell me?" he asked.

She bit her lip and lifted her hands in a helpless gesture.

"How could you?" he ground out. Fury rose up so strong in him, he felt his hands clench into fists. He stalked to the door and left before he said or did something he'd regret.

That night, Sandy called him. He thought about not

picking up, but if something had happened to Miranda, he wanted to know.

It seemed Miranda's mother wasn't so good at communicating.

Sandy wanted to come for a visit.

"To Charleston? Is Miranda all right?"

"Yes."

"Just say what you want to say, Sandy. You don't need to drive here."

"Yes, I do, now tell me where you live."

He'd given her his address and brief directions where he lived, then he'd worn a rut in the floor waiting for her to arrive. When the doorbell rang, he was already in the foyer, and had the door open.

"Oh." Sandy stepped inside. "Thank you, Nick."

"Want something to drink?"

"No. No. I'm sure you just want me to spit it out."

Good manners nudged him to lead her into the living room. He gestured for her to sit down.

"Let me start off by saying Tamara loves you. You know that, right?"

"This is probably a conversation I should be having with her."

"Except as you've noticed, she's tight-lipped. She's uncomfortable with matters of the heart. It's her analytical mind and her medical training. She doesn't do feeling so well. Well, that's not exactly true. She feels, but she has trouble expressing it."

"So what, you and Charlotte are acting as the go-between? If I want to find anything out, I'm going to have to ask one of you?" Nick ran his fingers through his hair in annoyance. "That's not going to work."

"There's more to it than that. Did Tamara ever tell you about her father?"

"No."

"Tamara was unplanned. Her father married me because his parents pressured him into doing the right thing, so we did. And he felt trapped. There wasn't a day that went by that he didn't resent me and Tamara for it. We finally divorced when she was 12." Sandy's pleading eyes sought his. "It was a relief, really. But those kinds of things, they shape a person, you know? Tamara is a beautiful, intelligent woman, but she's never been comfortable around men, and I think it's because of all of that baggage with her father. So, can you see why she wouldn't want to put herself or the baby in that same position?"

"She deliberately misled me. I specifically asked her about birth control. She knew she could get pregnant. She knew…. it."

Tamara's voice entered his mind. They'd been in the hotel room.

If my daughter died, I don't think I'd want to live. Her hand gripped his, the fire in her eyes intense. *I'd want to die, too. I would do anything if it meant she could live.*

I'd do anything if it meant she could live.

At the time she didn't think he was going to help her. He'd blown her off at his office and hadn't replied to the pictures she'd sent of Miranda through the mail.

And later when she'd told him she was pregnant, she'd said she had an alternative plan—a baby that would be a close genetic match.

What better chance for a close genetic match than for Nick to father a child?

Tamara hadn't slept with him to convince him to donate marrow. She'd slept with him because if he didn't donate the marrow, she'd have a chance at using the cord blood from the baby.

My God, it all made so much sense now. Why hadn't he realized it before?

Chapter Sixteen

Fred Thomas examined Miranda and stood next to the hospital bed smiling down at her. "Ready for that sherbie float, young lady? You can't have anything after midnight, so if you want one, this is the time to say so."

"Yes."

He nodded and looked at the nurse. "Brooke, call the kitchen and see what they can do about blended sherbet and sprite in a big cup for the patient."

The nurse nodded and walked out, and Stephen Travis, a hematologist, walked in.

What was he doing here? He walked toward her with his hand outraised. "Hi, Tamara. How are you?"

"Hi, Stephen. What are you doing here?" Panic rose quickly in her chest. "Something's wrong. What is it?"

Dr. Thomas leaned against the counter and crossed his arms. He grinned at Tamara. "Nothing's wrong. Everything is going very well, actually."

"Her blood count is up, yes, I saw."

"Even better news than that," Dr. Travis said.

"What?"

"We found a donor."

Simultaneous yelps of joy escaped her and Sandy's lips.

"Oh, thank God. Thank God." Sandy raised her hands in triumph.

"Are you sure?" Tamara asked.

Stephen nodded. "Yes. The lab contacted me about a possible match, but I wanted to make sure, so I requested a second sample. The sample came in Friday afternoon, and it looks perfect. Ten out of ten."

"Oh, my gosh. I can't believe it. I can't believe it."

"What's it mean, Mommy?"

Tamara sat on her daughter's bed and kissed her on the cheek. "It means you're going to get better."

"Of course, Miranda has nine more treatments first, but at the conclusion of the last treatment, we'll infuse the marrow and…." Dr. Travis laughed and shrugged. "hopefully get a complete remission."

"It's good news. Such good news!" Sandy began to cry.

The two men left, and without thinking Tamara pulled out her cell phone and texted Nick.

Found a bone marrow donor for Miranda

The second she sent it, horror at what she'd done blanketed her. Nick didn't want to hear from her. He was angry and upset. He'd found out she'd tricked him, trapped him into having a baby with her. Because of her conniving, they were going to have a connection forever, even if he chose not to acknowledge it.

She wouldn't hold him responsible.

I did this. Me.

Her phone rang. Nick. She slid the screen and held it to her ear, but she couldn't speak, whether it was joy, relief, guilt, or resignation, she didn't know.

"Tamara? Are you there?"

Her throat closed up, and she made a sound as if she were drowning.

"Sweetheart," he said, his voice so thick with emotion, it undid her.

"Nick. Oh, Nick."

"I know. I know. Devon and I will come over. Is she up for a visit tonight?"

"Uh-huh," was all Tamara could manage. She wanted to tell him she was sorry, ask him to forgive her, tell him he didn't owe her anything, but none of it would come.

"Thank you for telling me. We'll be there soon, and it will be all right."

They arrived, Devon pulling a string connected to a large Mylar balloon shaped like a cartoon poodle. Miranda squealed with delight when she saw it. She insisted she wanted to walk the dog around the room.

Tamara finally found the courage to look at Nick, but his attention was on Miranda as she jerked the balloon around making it do tricks.

"Man, it's hot in here," Devon said. He shed his jacket and laid it on one of the chairs in the room. "What are you guys trying to do...."

Devon continued speaking, but Tamara focused instead on his uncasted arm. She walked over to him and pulled at his hand.

"What is this?" she asked indicating the bruises she saw there. She ran her finger up his forearm and the puncture wound at the fold in his elbow. When she noticed the second, older, puncture, she looked up at his face and saw the practiced expression of innocence. No *what are you doing, Tamara?* No *hey what's the big idea?* Just a sincere I am completely clueless as to why you're looking at my arm.

A tiny bud of unease erupted into rage and she glared up at him. Without a word, she clenched his shirt and pulled him toward the door, leading him down the hall into the family conference room.

"Tamara? Tamara, where are you taking him?" she heard Nick call, his voice following them down the hall.

Inside the room, Tamara shoved Devon hard out of the doorway. Nick walked in. "What happened?" Nick asked, his face a kaleidoscope of emotion.

Tamara pushed Nick further into the room and shut the door, leaning against it. She pointed a finger at the teenager.

"Your father and I both told you no," she snapped.

"No to what? What the hell is going on here?"

"Your son underwent a test to see if he was a match for the bone marrow."

Devon stood there, watching Tamara steadily.

"Well?" she snapped.

He shrugged.

"How could you get away with this? They have your

medical records here. They know you're underage."

"My buddy Mitch is 18. We used his info to fill out the form, then when they called him, I went back. When they called him again, I gave blood again."

"It's all right, Dev. Go on back to the room. We'll be along in a minute," Nick said.

Tamara's attention swung to Nick. How could he be so calm? Devon walked out of the room, and the door shut softly behind him.

They had been so close. So close! But now they weren't going to be able to use the marrow because it was Devon's. Grief so strong pulled at Tamara. Emotion clogged her throat, her pores, her mouth. She reached her hands up and covered her face.

Nick's arms came around her, and he pulled her to him. His warmth surrounded her, but the chill of disappointment and hopelessness was too much.

She became aware that they sat on the small couch in the room. He'd pulled her across his body, tucked her face into his chest, his hand roving over her as if he were comforting Miranda. The wave of tears subsided, and she took a shuddering breath.

"I almost never cry," Tamara said. Only maybe four times total. Two of them with Nick.

"It's probably the hormones from the baby," he said matter of factly.

"How could he go behind our backs and commit medical forgery?"

"Because he's 16 and defiant."

Tamara raised her head and looked at him, shocked at how calm he was.

"I knew he did it, by the way. He told me on the way over here."

"You knew?"

"Yeah." His mouth turned up on one side, as if he'd just remembered a joke.

"But…" Tamara shook her head. "He can't do it, Nick,

even though the transplant can't happen for five months and he'll be 17."

"He can if I grant permission."

"But you're not going to do that. He's too young. There's a risk...."

"But it's a small risk. You said so yourself. He really wants to do it. It will save Miranda's life, and I am really proud of him for going forward even if he did disobey me to do it. It's the right thing to do."

Tamara tried to take it in. Nick knew, and he was okay with this? She shook her head. "No. I will not allow...."

Nick laughed, tightened his arm around her, and dropped a kiss on top of her head. "You're not the doctor who gets to say. You are the recipient's mother. These things tend to be anonymous, and would have been probably except for three things. First, your admirable skills of observation, second, how hot-natured Devon is."

"What's number three?"

"You're probably going to notice when Devon has the bone marrow removed because I plan on us being engaged by then. How do you feel about having a 16 year old defiant stepson, Dr. Badass?"

She couldn't have heard him right. Tamara searched his face in an attempt to fathom his meaning, his emotion— anything—that would help her make sense of his words. "Engaged? I'm not....I'm not marrying you."

"Why not?"

"Because I tricked you. You didn't want a baby. You just wanted one night in a hotel with a stranger who liked the same movie as you. I'm not holding you responsible for me or...or a baby or anything."

Nick sighed. He patted her shoulder. "Okay. Fine. No engagement. No marriage. No obligation. No nothing if you can answer one question correctly." He lowered his chin, pinning her with his emerald eyes. "Honestly. Do you love me?"

Yes! Tamara blinked at him. "We've only known

each...."

"Ah, ah, ah, ah, ah," returning to her the same silencing treatment she'd given him once. "Yes or no. Only. Do you love me?"

Tamara huffed. "Yes."

"See? That wasn't so hard to say, was it?" He smiled, and his gaze softened. "It's the wrong answer, by the way. You only get out of marrying me if the answer had been no."

"This isn't the 1950s. Just because I'm pregnant does not mean we should get married. That's stupid, Nick."

"Except I love you, and I love Miranda, and you love me. And Devon. He's crazy about you. He's finally opening up to me. Things are better with us than they've ever been."

"I'm glad you and Devon are getting along. But, I'm not marrying you."

"We'll see."

****

Tamara sat next to Miranda's hospital bed and watched her daughter. Though Miranda had completed the chemotherapy, she looked much sicker than when they began months ago. She had received Devon's marrow, and if her blood levels continued to improve, she would go home later today.

A knock sounded on the door, and Devon walked in alone. He must have seen Tamara glance behind him. "Dad's not with me."

"Oh."

Miranda stirred in her sleep.

"Sorry." Devon lowered his voice. His troubled gaze studied the child. "How is she?"

"Her color's a little better, and her red blood count is up."

Devon stood uncertainly, and Tamara waved him toward the couch. With a little difficulty because she was almost in her third trimester, she turned the chair she sat on so it faced where he settled himself.

Tamara watched him closely for any signs of discomfort.

Though it had been weeks since his procedure, he'd developed an infection, scaring her. "How are you feeling?"

"Great."

"Really?"

He grinned. "Really, and, no, you can't take my temperature. I'm fine. What about you, you doing okay? Carrying a baby's a lot more stress than a couple of little holes in my hip bone."

She nodded her head in acknowledgement. "Does your dad know you're here?"

"Yeah. I texted him. I told him I wanted to hang out here until Little B.A. goes home."

"Her immune system is stronger than it was, but we want to be very cautious."

"Dad says he's coming over after work." Uneasiness thundered over the young man's face, then it was gone. Any time Nick came over, Tamara insisted Devon have an invite as well. It had made any late night trysts between Nick and Tamara less frequent, though Devon did not accompany his dad every time.

"Maybe you two would like to stay the night at the house."

Devon blinked at her.

"Sandy and I decided we'd like to give you the guestroom. You could fix it up as you like, and any time you want to come over and stay the night, you could."

"Does Dad know?"

"I talked to him about it, yes."

"What did he say?"

"He thought it was a great idea."

His exact response had been a mock scowl. *You never let me spend the night*, he'd said.

That's because you have a son at home alone, Tamara had countered.

The scowl transformed into a lecherous grin. *So if he stays the night, so could I.*

Devon's eyebrow went up along with one corner of his

mouth. "Guess it's none of my business where Dad sleeps."

"We've got two couches in the house. He'll be okay."

"Right." Devon laughed. "Badass, they've got a daycare at my school for all of the teen parents. You guys really need to set a better example."

Tamara's smile fell. "Devon, to be totally honest, I will likely sleep in Miranda's room tonight. I'm not saying that will be the case every night, but, you and your dad have become part of Miranda's life—and mine—and, well, I want you to know you have a place at my house."

Devon gestured to Tamara's stomach. "What about little baby bad ass? Dad hasn't said it, but he's way too involved for me to believe you went to a sperm bank this time."

"No, I didn't. But I would not have gotten pregnant if I couldn't raise and support the baby myself. I was forty when Miranda was born, and even though I wish I could have found someone to love and marry first, that wasn't an option for me."

Devon crooked his head. "Marrying my dad isn't an option now?"

Embarrassment caused Tamara to stumble over her words. "I don't want him to feel as if he has to."

"He doesn't."

"Has he talked to you about this?"

"Not really. A few questions here and there. How would I feel if he got married again, would I be open to going to a new school if we moved, things like that which make me think he's thinking about it."

Nick was definitely thinking about it. He'd wanted to go shopping for rings on Valentine's Day, and Tamara adamantly refused. Getting Miranda well and preparing for the baby—that's all Tamara could focus on for now.

The baby kicked her, as if she knew Tamara was thinking about her.

"How would you feel about it, your dad getting married again, moving to another city, another school?"

"If he was getting married to you, you mean?" His eyes

narrowed, and he stared at Tamara until she had to work not to squirm.

She nodded once.

"Look, Tamara, I wanted to do what I did—the bone marrow. I wanted to do that, okay?"

"All right."

"You didn't ask me to. I know you appreciate it, especially if it helps Little Bad Ass over there."

"I do appreciate it. Devon, you've saved her life. I'll never forget what you've—"

He held up his hand. "Okay. Okay. Okay. Well, if you really appreciate it, then I think you can marry him. My dad."

What? Surely, she didn't hear him right.

"You want me to thank you by marrying your dad?"

Devon grinned. "Pretty much. Yes."

Tamara shook her head. "I don't.... Devon, we—Nick and I—can't get married just because you want it."

"No, not just because I want it."

He let those words sink in.

Tamara sat back. The little manipulator. "Are you blackmailing me?"

"No ma'am. I am simply casting my vote. We live in a democracy, after all, and I bet if we ask Miranda, she'll vote along the same party lines as me."

Tamara pursed her lips. "Neither one of you are old enough to vote."

"What about Sandy? What would her vote be, do you think?"

"Why do you care, Devon?"

"Because you do. You don't have to care about me, but you do. My blood is in her now. We're joined by blood. All of us. You and Dad need to make it official. Tell him you'll marry him."

The door opened, and Nick walked in. He bent over the bed, looked Miranda over, picked up her hand, kissed it, then came to where Tamara and Devon sat.

"Hi." He looked at Tamara then at Devon. "What?"

"Tamara has something to tell you," Devon said.

Nick turned to her, his gaze darkening with anxiety. "What's wrong?"

Tamara cleared her throat. "Devon thinks we should get married."

"Really?" His lips quirked upward. "You sure you want her as a stepmother? She's a lot meaner than I am."

"He's serious, Nick," Tamara snapped.

Nick gestured to her as if her statement proved his point.

She shook her head in disgust and tried to stand up, but it wasn't easy, and it just made her even angrier. Nick lifted her gently, then his arms tightened around her.

He kissed the tip of her nose. "I'm sorry."

"For what?"

"For saying you're mean. I would love to marry you. Just say when."

"Before school starts," Devon said.

"I was asking her," Nick said without breaking eye contact with Tamara. "When would suit you?"

Tamara turned and looked at Miranda. "When she's well enough. Mid-September perhaps. She'll have her strength back by then."

"Mid-September." Nick nodded.

"Dad, you better get something in writing so she doesn't back out."

"I imagine once Miranda finds out, she's not going to let her mom back out."

"I'm not the pushover where Miranda is concerned," Tamara groused.

"No, apparently, only where Devon is concerned." Nick indicated the teen with a nod of his head. "But, that's okay with me." His green eyes sparkled down at her, love evident in them.

The End

AUTHOR'S NOTE

"She is more righteous than I."

Genesis 38: 26

This is a Bible story. Sort of.

The inspiration for this book came from a somewhat obscure story in Genesis 38 in which a desperate widow engages in a plan to have a baby.

One thing to understand in the ancient Biblical culture is how much a child—especially a son—means to a woman. In a time before social security and retirement and women in the workplace, a woman depended on her adult children for survival in her old age. Not only that, but people considered their legacy to be their children. If a woman was not able to get pregnant, she was considered cursed. Obviously, she or her husband had done something wrong to deserve the disgrace of infertility. Now, there are hints in Scripture that this wasn't actually true, but overall, I contend it was an agreed upon cultural more.

So, this man—Er—marries Tamar. But he is wicked and he dies.

In the ancient Jewish culture, if a husband dies before he has fathered a child, it is the duty of the closest male relative (usually the man's brother) to have sex with the widow for the sole purpose of producing a child who would be considered the offspring of the dead man. This is known as Levirate law. Judah, Er's father, sends his second son to perform this duty. But Scripture tells us that every time he had sex with Tamar, he would spill "his semen on the ground to keep from providing offspring for his brother" (Genesis 38:9).

Can you imagine how awful this was for Tamar? She's lost her husband, and now she must endure sex with his brother, but because he pulls out before he ejaculates, she knows the act is fruitless. What a horrible, horrible thing.

Where is the justice?

God provides it, apparently, by putting this brother to death.

And there is one more son, but Judah refuses to give him to Tamar though the Levirate law requires it. Judah has already lost two of his sons. He doesn't want to lose his third son. And he obviously thinks Tamar is somehow to blame. Time passes, and still he puts off sending his only remaining son to Tamar. Judah's wife dies, and he is left as a widower. More time passes.

And Tamar still does not have the child she so desperately desires to secure her future.

So, she disguises herself as a prostitute and waits where she knows Judah will travel on a trip he is making. The disguise must have been a good one, and alluring as well for Judah receives what she offers, but he has no money, so instead he leaves his seal, cord, and staff as a pledge for payment. Later Judah sends his servant to pay the prostitute, but—uh oh, she's disappeared, and the talk in town is there are no prostitutes on that road anyway. Judah tells his servant to forget about it since it could be a source of embarrassment for him.

After leaving the road, Tamar puts on her widow's clothes once again. Her scheme has worked, and she's pregnant. Judah finds out Tamar is pregnant and the rumor is she has been prostituting. He demands she is to be burned to death for her crime. But Tamar—that clever woman—sends to him his staff and seal with a message. "I am pregnant by the man who owns these. See if you recognize whose seal and cord and staff these are."

Of course, Judah recognizes his own things. He realizes he hasn't treated Tamar justly according to the Levirate law, and he says of her, "She is more righteous than I." Interestingly, Scripture tells us that Judah never slept with her again. I think this is to show us that it really was about duty and not about the sex.

Tamar is some woman. The lengths that she goes to so that she can have a child and how she outsmarts her father-in-law inspired me. But there's a seediness to this old tale, so I wanted to clean it up a bit. The hero I created wouldn't visit a prostitute, so I changed that detail.

Also, there was an *ICK* factor of father and son having sex with the same woman. How could I get around that? Modern medicine, of course, which is why my heroine visits a sperm bank.

And I had to give my heroine—Tamara (see the resemblance to Tamar's name?)—a really, really good reason to seduce a man, and, in effect, steal his baby. If the Levirate law is to be sure the first man has an offspring, I decided that if Tamara already has a child who could die, then tricking Nick into having sex with her to save that child's life could work. But, it seemed too easy if not only did she get pregnant the one time, but also that the baby would be a perfect donor match. I mean, how much could I indulge in the reader's suspension of disbelief? Besides, in the Biblical version, there's a son who has been withheld from performing the duty. So, what if there was another son that Tamara didn't know about? Thus, Devon is part of my story, too.

In my story, the Tamar and Judah characters end up together with a pledge to be husband and wife. In my story, the baby is loved and wanted not just as a plan for retirement, but as a cherished child. I love that my hero, Nick, finds healing and forgiveness through Tamara's desperation to save her daughter's life. I love that a family is created and will be together. I hope you enjoyed reading this story as much as I enjoyed writing it.

Did you know there is another book available in the Family Tangles series?

It's called *Faithful*, and it is a modern telling of Jacob, Leah, and Rachel, a Biblical story found in Genesis. It always bothered me that Leah and Rachel who were sisters competed with each other for the love of Jacob, so in my story their love and devotion for each other is just as important as the relationship with the man in their lives, and Jacob is faithful to his wife. That was important to me, too.

Here's an excerpt:

"What do you think about having Noel's baby?"

Nila stared at her twin waiting for the punch line, examining the face so much like her own for a hint of mirth. Nothing.

"I think it would be weird since he's your husband." Noel also happened to be Nila's best guy friend and her brother-in-law.

"I need you to get over the weirdness, Nila. Dr. Garber has scheduled me for a hysterectomy next month."

"Lil! Why didn't you tell me?"

Lil had never been on birth control in the seven years she and Noel had been married. In the last year, they had been trying in earnest to conceive with no success. When Lil began having severe abdominal pain, she had gone to see her OB/GYN.

"I am telling you."

"Is it…?" Nila couldn't make herself say the word.

Lil gazed out the window, tears filling her eyes.

"Lil!"

"No."

"Lil, please. It's not...?" Nila begged.

"It's just a uterine tumor."

"Just a uterine tumor? *Just* a uterine tumor? Does Noel know?"

"Not yet."

"Geez, Lil!"

"It would be a good idea for you to get checked out though. As soon as you can, just in case."

Lil stood up and walked over to the counter pulling a tissue out of its decorative box and touching it to the corner of each eye. She sniffed and glanced up at the ceiling. Nila studied the woman.

"Are you sure it isn't cancer?" Finally, Nila pushed that word past her lips, the disease that had killed their mother after she had suffered round after round of chemotherapy. "I mean, a tumor usually means cancer. Right?"

"They're going to run a few tests, but the doctor says the shape of the tumor indicates it is fibroid and non-cancerous. The surgery will take care of it." She squared her shoulders and sniffed again. "But not the problem of Junior." Sitting back down across from her sister, she grasped her hands. "I can't have him now, so I need you to do it for me."

"You guys are on the adoption list, Lil. You should give it time."

Lil snorted. "Three years on the off chance we'll be approved?"

"Well, it's not the end of the world if you can't have kids. Lots of people don't have kids, and they do fine."

"But we want kids. We really want them. Noel..." Lil gave a watery laugh. "Noel opened a college account. Did I tell you? He's determined the baby's going to UK."

The back door opened, and Noel walked in. When he saw the two women, he stopped. Looking from one to the other, his expression turned to stone. Nila sat back as the charged air shot back and forth between husband and wife.

"Oh, Noel!" Lil sobbed. He was across the room within a second, and she launched herself into his arms.

Noel held her head to his chest and buried his face in her hair. Anguish ripped at Nila's heart. She shoved her chair back, picked up her purse, and walked out of the house not wanting to impose on this private moment between Lil and Noel.

By the time she got to her car, Nila's breaths were coming in short gasps. She sat in her car working to unclench her teeth. She beat on the steering wheel a few times.

It should have been me. My uterus with the damn tumor in it!

What did she need her uterus for anyway? It's not like any man would ever want to have a baby with her.

You can find *Faithful* at most online bookstores or in print at Amazon. You can go to my website for the link to purchase it.

There is a third book in the Tangled Family series called *Steadfast*. If you are interested in knowing when it is released, please send me an email, and I will let you know.
My email is **booksbyjenniferjohnson@gmail.com**

About Jennifer Johnson

Who am I?

I am a writer.

I write contemporary romantic fiction.

I aspire to be Wonder Woman with the awesome leotard and the criminal-fighting boots on some days. On other days I am Wonder Woman with my lasso of Truth and my no-nonsense-pursuit of justice.

I live in the South across the river from the Midwest. I'm married to Super Man with a Tony Stark mind. We have Wonder/Super children and a bionic dog. All in all, it's a comic book kind of life.

You can find out more about me at my website **www.booksbyjenniferjohnson.com** and connect with me on Facebook at **https://www.facebook.com/booksbyjenniferjohnson** and through Twitter at **https://twitter.com/BooksbyJennifer**